S0-HIQ-113

William Hays Hindley
Bellhaven
N. C.
1915

JOHN L. STODDARD'S LECTURES

SOUTHERN CALIFORNIA

GRAND CAÑON OF THE COLORADO RIVER

YELLOWSTONE NATIONAL PARK

Norwood Press
J. S. Cushing Co. — Berwick & Smith Co.
Norwood, Mass., U.S.A.

Boston Bookbinding Co., Cambridge, Mass.

The Engravings are by John Andrew & Son, Boston

ELECTRIC PEAK.

JOHN L. STODDARD'S LECTURES

COMPLETE IN TEN VOLUMES

VOLUME TEN

CHICAGO & BOSTON
GEO. L. SHUMAN & CO.
MCMXV

SOUTHERN CALIFORNIA

PACHANGO INDIANS AT HOME.

SOUTHERN CALIFORNIA

NATURE has carefully guarded Southern California. Ten thousand miles of ocean roll between her western boundary and the nearest continent; while eastward, her divinity is hedged by dreary deserts that forbid approach. Although the arid plains of eastern Arizona are frequently called deserts, it is not till the west-bound tourist has passed Flagstaff that the word acquires a real and terrible significance. Then, during almost an entire day he journeys through a region which, while it fascinates, inspires him with dread. Occasionally a flock of goats suggests the possibility of sustaining life here, but sometimes for a distance of

LIFE ON THE DESERT.

THE DESERT'S MOUNTAINS.

fifty miles he may see neither man nor beast. The villages, if such they can be called, are merely clusters of rude huts dotting an area of rocky desolation. No trees are visible. No grazing-ground relieves the dismal monochrome of sand. The mountains stand forth dreary, gaunt, and naked. In one locality the train runs through a series of gorges the sides of which are covered with disintegrated rock, heaped up in infinite confusion, as if an awful ague-fit had seized the hills, and shaken them until their ledges had been broken into a million boulders. At another point, emerging from a maze of mountains, the locomotive shoots into a plain, forty or fifty miles square, and sentineled on every side by savage peaks. Once, doubtless, an enormous lake was held encompassed by these giants; but, taking advantage of some seismic agitation, it finally slipped through their fingers to the sea, and now men travel over its deserted bed. Sometimes these monsters seemed to be closing in upon us, as if to thwart our exit and crush us in their stony arms; but the resistless steed that bore us onward, though quivering and panting with the effort, always contrived to find the narrow opening toward liberty. Occasionally our route lay through enormous fields of cactus and yucca trees, twelve feet in height, and, usually, so hideous from their distorted shapes and prickly spikes, that I could understand the proverb, "Even the Devil cannot eat a cactus."

As the day wore on, and we were drawn from one scene of desolation to another, I almost doubted, like Bunyan's Pilgrim, whether we should ever reach the promised land alive; but, finally, through a last upheaval of defiant hills which were, if possible, more desolate and weird than any we had seen, we gained the boundary of California and gazed upon the Colorado River. It is a stream whose history thrilled me as I remembered how in its long and tortuous course of more than a thousand miles to this point it had laboriously cut its way through countless desert cañons, and I felt glad to see it here at last,

DESERT VEGETATION.

sweeping along in tranquil majesty as if aware that all its struggles were now ended, and peace and victory had been secured.

It was sunset when our train, having crossed this river, ran along its western bank to our first stopping-place in California, — the Needles. Never shall I forget the impression made upon me as I looked back toward the wilderness from which we had emerged. What! was that it — that vision of transfiguration — that illumined Zion radiant with splendor? Across the river, lighted by the evening's after-glow of fire, rose a celestial city, with towers, spires, and battlements glittering as if sheathed in burnished gold. Sunshine and distance had dispelled all traces of the region's barrenness, and for a few memorable moments, while we watched it breathlessly, its sparkling bastions seemed to beckon us alluringly to its magnificence; then, fading like an exquisite mirage created by the genii of the desert, it swiftly sank into the desolation from which the sun had summoned it, to crown it briefly with supernal glory. Turning at last from its cold immobility to the activity around us, I saw some representatives of the fallen race of

LOOKING BACK AT THE MOUNTAINS.

A CALIFORNIA RANCH SCENE.

INDIAN HUTS.

California, as Indian bucks and squaws came from their squalid hovels to sell the trifling products of their industry, and stare at what to them is a perpetual miracle, — the passing train. Five races met upon that railroad platform, and together illustrated the history of the country. First, in respect to time, was the poor Indian, slovenly, painted and degraded, yet characterized by a kind of bovine melancholy on the faces of the men, and a trace of animal beauty in the forms of the young squaws. Teasing and jesting with the latter were the negro

"A FALLEN RACE."

porters of the train, who, though their ancestors were as little civilized as those of the Indians, have risen to a level only to be appreciated by comparing the African and the Indian side by side. There, also, was the Mexican, the lord of all this region in his earlier and better days, but now a penniless degenerate of Old Castile. Among them stood the masterful Anglo-Saxon, whose energy has pushed aside the Spaniard, civilized the Negro, developed half a continent, built this amazing path of steel through fifteen hundred miles of desert, and who is king wherever he goes. While I surveyed these specimens of humanity and compared them, one with another, there suddenly appeared among them a fifth figure, — that of Sing Lee, formerly a subject of the oldest government on earth, and still a representative of the four hundred millions swarming in the Flowery Kingdom. Strangely enough, of all these different racial types, the Mongol seemed the most self-satisfied. The Yankee was continually bustling about, feeding passengers, transporting trunks, or hammering car-wheels; the Negroes were joking with the Indians, who appeared stolidly apathetic or resigned; the Mexicans stood apart in sullen gloom, as if secretly

A MEXICAN HOUSE AND FAMILY

THE BLOSSOMING WILDERNESS.

X. — I

COMPLACENT MONGOLS.

mourning their lost estate; but Sing Lee looked about him with a cheerful calmness which seemed indicative of absolute contentment and his face wore, continually, a complacent smile. What strange varieties of human destiny these men present, I thought as I surveyed them: the Indian and the Mexican stand for the hopeless Past; the Anglo-Saxon and the Negro for the active Present; while Sing Lee is a specimen of that yellow race which is embalmed in its own conservatism, like a fly in amber.

The unsuspecting traveler who has crossed the Colorado River and entered Southern California, naturally looks around him for the orange groves of which he has so often heard, and is astonished not to find himself surrounded by them; but, gradually, the truth is forced upon his mind that, in this section of our country, he must not base his calculations upon

CHARACTERISTIC SCENERY

STRIKING CONTRASTS.

eastern distances, or eastern areas. For, even after he has passed the wilderness of Arizona and the California frontier, he discovers that the Eldorado of his dreams lies on the other side of a desert, two hundred miles in breadth, beyond whose desolate expanse the siren of the Sunset Sea still beckons him and whispers: "This is the final barrier; cross it, and I am yours." The transit is not difficult, however, in days like these; for the whole distance from Chicago to the coast can be accomplished in sixty-seven hours, and where the transcontinental traveler of less than half a century ago was threatened day and night with attacks from murderous Apaches, and ran the risk of perishing of thirst in many a waterless "Valley of Death," the modern tourist sleeps securely in a Pullman car, is waited on by a colored servant, and dines in railway restaurants the management of which, both in the quality and quantity of the food supplied, even in the heart of the Great American Desert, is justly famous for its excellence.

At San Bernardino, we enter what is called the Garden of Southern California; but even here it is possible to be disappointed, if we expect to find the entire country an unbroken paradise of orange trees and roses. Thousands of oranges and lemons, it is true, suspend their miniature globes of gold against the sky; but interspersed between their groves are wastes of sand, reminding us that all the fertile portion of this region has been as truly wrested from the wilderness, as Holland from the sea. Accordingly, since San Bernardino County alone is twice as large as Massachusetts, and the County of Los Angeles nearly the size of Connecticut, it is not difficult to understand why a continuous expanse of verdure is not seen. The truth is, Southern California, with a few exceptions, is cultivated only where man has brought to it vivifying water. When that appears, life springs up from sterility, as water gushed forth from the rock in the Arabian desert when the great leader of the Israelites smote it in obedience to Divine command. Hence, there is always present here the fascination of the unattained, which yet is readily attainable, patiently waiting for the master-hand that shall unlock the sand-roofed treasure-houses of fertility with a crystal key. It can be easily imagined, therefore, that this is a land of striking contrasts.

WRESTED FROM THE SAND.

Pass, for example, through the suburbs of Los Angeles, and you will find that, while one yard is dry and bare, the next may be embellished with a palm tree twenty feet in height, with roses clambering over the portico of the house, and lilies blooming in the garden. Of the three things essential to vegetation — soil, sun, and water — man must contribute (and it is all he can contribute) water.

Once let the tourist here appreciate the fact that almost all the verdure which delights his eyes is the gift of water at the hand of man, and any disappointment he may have at first experienced will be changed to admiration. Moreover, with the least encouragement this country bursts forth into verdure, crowns its responsive soil with fertility, and smiles with bloom. Even the slightest tract of herbage, however brown it may be in the dry season, will in the springtime clothe itself with green, and decorate its emerald robe with spangled flowers. In fact, the wonderful profusion of wild flowers, which, when the winter rains have saturated the ground, transform these hillsides into floral terraces, can never be too highly praised. Happy is he

A PALM-GIRT AVENUE, LOS ANGELES.

AN ARBOR IN WINTER.

who visits either Palestine or Southern California when they are bright with blossoms and redolent of fragrance. The climax of this renaissance of Nature is, usually, reached about the middle of April, but in proportion as the rain comes earlier or later, the season varies slightly. At a time when many cities of the North and East are held in the tenacious grip of winter, their gray skies thick with soot, their pavements deep in slush, and their inhabitants clad in furs, the cities of Southern California celebrate their floral carnival, which is a time of great rejoicing, attended with an almost fabulous display of flowers. Los Angeles, for example, has expended as much as twenty-five thousand dollars on the details of one such festival. The entire city is then gay with flags and banners, and in the long procession horses, carriages, and riders are so profusely decked with flowers, that they resemble a slowly moving throng of animated bouquets. Ten thousand choice roses have been at such times fastened to the wheels, body, pole, and harness of a single equipage. Sometimes the individual exhibitions in these floral pageants take the form of floats, which represent all sorts of myths and allegories, portrayed elaborately by means of statues, as well as living beings, lavishly adorned with ornamental grasses, and wild and cultivated flowers.

Southern California is not only a locality, it is a type. It cannot be defined by merely mentioning parallels of latitude. We think of it and love it as the dreamland of the Spanish Missions, and as a region rescued from aridity, and made a home for the invalid and the winter tourist. Los Angeles is really its metropolis, but San Diego, Pasadena, and Santa Barbara are prosperous and progressive cities whose population increases only less rapidly than their ambition.

One of the first things for an eastern visitor to do, on arriving at Los Angeles, is to take the soft sound of *g* out of the city's name, and to remember that the Spaniards and Mexicans pronounce *e* like the English *a* in fate. This is not absolutely necessary for entrance into good society, but the pronunciation "Angeelees" is tabooed. The first Anglo-Saxon to arrive here was brought by the Mexicans, in 1822, as a prisoner. Soon after, however, Americans appeared in constantly increasing numbers, and, on August 13, 1846, Major Fremont raised at

MAIN STREET, LOS ANGELES.

FREMONT'S HEADQUARTERS.

Los Angeles the Stars and Stripes, and the house that he occupied may still be seen. Nevertheless, the importance of Los Angeles is of recent date. In 1885 it was an adobe village, dedicated to the Queen of the Angels; to-day, a city of brick and stone, with three hundred thousand inhabitants, it calls

PALATIAL RESIDENCES IN LOS ANGELES.

LOS ANGELES.

itself the Queen of the State. Its streets are broad, many of its buildings are massive and imposing, and its fine residences beautiful. It is the capital of Southern California, and the headquarters of its fruit-culture. The plains and valleys surrounding it are one mass of vineyards, orange groves and orchards, and, in one year, the value of oranges alone exported from this city has amounted to twenty-five millions of dollars! There is, however, less verdure here than in well-cared-for eastern towns of corresponding size, and Los Angeles, and even Pasadena, notwithstanding their many palm trees, have on the whole a bare appearance, compared with a city like New Haven, with its majestic elms and robe of vivid green, which even in autumn seems to dream of summer bloom. Nevertheless, Los Angeles is clean, and poverty and squalor rarely show themselves; while, in the suburbs of the city, even the humblest dwellings are frequently surrounded by palm trees, and made beautiful by flowers.

Another charm of Los Angeles is the sudden contrasts it presents. Thus, a short ride from his hotel will bring the tourist to the remains of the humble Mexican village which was the forerunner of the present city. There he will find the inevitable Plaza with its little park and fountain, without which no Mexican town is complete. There, too, is the characteristic adobe church, the quaint interior of which presents a curious medley of old weather-beaten statues and modern furniture, and is always pervaded by that smell peculiar to long-inhabited adobe buildings, and which is called by Steele, in his charming "Old California Days," the national odor of Mexico.

Los Angeles, also, has its Chinatown, which in its manners and customs is, fortunately, as distinct from the American portion of the city as if it were an island in the Pacific; but it gave me an odd sensation to be able to pass at once from the handsome, active settlement of the Anglo-Saxon into the stupidity of Mexico, or the heathenism of China.

PLAZA AND ADOBE CHURCH, LOS ANGELES.

BROADWAY, LOS ANGELES.

"How can I distinguish here a native Californian from an eastern man?" I asked a resident.

"There are no native Californians," was the somewhat exaggerated reply; "this is not only a modern, but an eastern city. Nine-tenths of our inhabitants came here from the East less than a quarter of a century ago. We are an old people with a new home."

Ostrich rearing is now a profitable industry of California, and farms have been established for this purpose at half a dozen points in the southern section of the State. Two of them are in the vicinity of Los Angeles, and well repay a visit; for, if one is unacquainted with the habits of these graceful birds, there is instruction as well as amusement in studying their appearance, character, and mode of life. My first view of the feathered bipeds was strikingly spectacular. As every one knows, the ostrich is decidedly *décolleté* as well as utterly indifferent to the covering of its legs. Accordingly a troop of them, as they came balancing and tiptoeing toward me, reminded me of a company of ballet dancers tripping down the stage. While the head of the ostrich is unusually small, its eyes are large and have an expression of mischief which gives warning of danger. During a visit to one of the farms, I saw a male bird pluck two hats from unwary men, and it looked wicked enough to have taken their heads as well, had they not been more securely fastened. It is sometimes sarcastically asserted that the ostrich digests with satisfaction to itself such articles as gimlets, nails, and penknives; but this is a slander. It needs gravel, like all creatures of its class which have to grind their food in an interior grist-mill; but though it will usually bite at any bright object, it will not always swallow it. I saw one peck at a ribbon on a lady's hat, and, also, at a pair of shears in its keeper's hands, but this was no proof that it intended to devour either. On another occasion, an ostrich snatched a purse from a lady's hand and instantly dropped it; but when a gold piece fell from it, the bird immediately swallowed that, showing how easily even animals fall under the influence of Californian lust for gold.

AN OSTRICH FARM.

Sixteen miles from Los Angeles, yet owing to the clear atmosphere, apparently, rising almost at the terminus of the city's streets, stand the Sierra Madre Mountains, whose copious reservoirs furnish this entire region with water. An excursion toward this noble range brought me one day to Pasadena, the pride of all the towns which, relatively to Los Angeles, resemble the satellites of a central sun. Pasadena seems a garden without a weed; a city without a hovel; a laughing, happy, prosperous, charming town, basking forever in the sunshine, and lying at the feet of still, white mountain peaks, whose cool breath moderates the semi-tropical heat of one of the most exquisitely beautiful valleys in the world. These mountains, although sombre and severe, are not so awful and forbidding as those of the Arizona desert, but they are notched and jagged, as their name *Sierra* indicates, and scars and gashes on their surfaces give proof of the terrific battles which they have waged for ages with

ORANGE GROVE AVENUE, PASADENA.

THREE MILES FROM ORANGES TO SNOW.

the elements. A striking feature of their scenery is that they rise so abruptly from the San Gabriel Valley, that from Pasadena one can look directly to their bases, and even ride to them in a trolley car; and the peculiar situation of the city is evidenced by the fact that, in midwinter, its residents, while picking oranges and roses in their gardens, often see snow-squalls raging on the neighboring peaks of the Sierra.

It would be difficult to overpraise the charm of Pasadena and its environs. Less than half a century ago the site of the present city was a sheep-pasture. To-day it boasts of a population of more than one hundred thousand souls, one hundred and fifty miles of well-paved streets, numerous handsome public buildings and hundreds of attractive homes. One of its streets is lined for a mile with specimens of the fan palm, fifteen feet in height; and I realized the prodigality of Nature here when my guide pointed out a heliotrope sixteen

A PASADENA HOTEL.

feet in height, covering the whole porch of a house; while, in driving through a private estate, I saw, in close proximity, sago and date palms, and lemon, orange, camphor, pepper, pomegranate, fig, quince, and walnut trees.

As we stood spellbound on the summit of Pasadena's famous Raymond Hill, below us lay the charming town, wrapped in the calm repose that distance always gives even to scenes of great activity; beyond this stretched away along the valley such an enchanting vista of green fields and golden flowers, and pretty houses nestling in foliage, and orchards bending 'neath their luscious fruits, that it appeared a veritable paradise; and the effect of light and color, the combination of perfect sunshine and well-tempered heat, the view in one direction of the ocean twenty miles away, and, in the other, of the range of the Sierra Madre only

A PASADENA RESIDENCE.

PASADENA.

seven miles distant, with the San Gabriel Valley sleeping at its base, produced a picture so divinely beautiful, that we were moved to smiles or tears with the unreasoning rapture of a child over these lavish gifts of Nature. Yet this same Nature has imposed an inexorable condition on the recipients of her bounty; for most of this luxuriance is dependent upon irrigation. "The palm," said my informant, "will grow with little moisture here, and so will barley and the grape-vine; but everything else needs water, which must be artificially supplied."

"How do you obtain it?" I asked.

"We buy the requisite amount of water with our land," was the reply. "Do you see that little pipe," he added, pointing to an orange grove, "and do you notice the furrows between the trees? Once in so often the water must be turned on there; and, as the land is sloping, the precious liquid gradually fills the trenches and finds its way to the roots of the trees."

Dealers in California wines declare that people ought to use

A RAISIN RANCH.

AN ORANGE GROVE, PASADENA.

them in preference to the imported vintage of Europe, and the warehouses they have built prove the sincerity of their conviction. One storehouse in the San Gabriel Valley is as large as the City Hall of New York, and contains wooden receptacles for wine rivaling in size the great tun of Heidelberg. We walked between its endless rows of hogsheads, filled with wine; and, finally, in the sample-room were invited to try in turn the claret, burgundy, sherry, port, and brandy.

"How much wine do you make?" I asked the gentleman in charge.

"In one year," was the reply, "we made a million gallons."

A CALIFORNIA VINEYARD.

I thought of the Los Angeles River which I had crossed that morning, and of its sandy bed one hundred feet in width, with a current in the centre hardly larger than the stream from a hose-pipe, and remarked, "Surely, in some portions of this land there is more wine than water." "Where do you sell it?" I presently inquired.

"Everywhere," was the answer, "even in France; and what goes over there you subsequently buy, at double the price, for real French wine."

It was the old story, and I doubt not there is truth in it; but the products of California vineyards, owing, possibly, to

AT THE BASE OF THE MOUNTAINS.

the very richness of the soil, do not seem to me to possess a flavor equal in delicacy to that of the best imported wines. This will, however, be remedied in time, and in the comparatively near future this may become the great wine-market of the world. Certainly no State in the Union has a climate better adapted to vine-growing, and there are now within its borders no less than ninety million vines, which yield grapes and raisins of the finest quality.

No visit to Pasadena would be complete without an excursion to the neighboring mountains, which not only furnish the inhabitants with water, but, also, contribute greatly to their happiness and recreation. For, having at last awakened to the fact that comfort and delight awaited them in the recesses and upon the summits of their giant hills, the Californians have built fine roads along the mountain sides, established camping-grounds and hostelries at several attractive points, and, finally, constructed a remarkable elevated railroad, by which the people of Los Angeles can, in three hours, reach the crest of the Sierra Madre, six thousand feet above the sea. Soon after leaving Pasadena, a trolley takes the tourist with great rapidity straight toward the mountain wall, which, though presenting at a distance the appearance of an unbroken rampart, disintegrates as he approaches it into separate peaks; so that the crevices, which look from Pasadena like mere wrinkles on the faces of these granite giants, prove upon close inspection to be cañons of considerable depth. I was surprised and charmed to see the amount of cultivation which is carried to the very bases of these cliffs. Orchards and orange groves approach the monsters fearlessly, and shyly drop golden fruit,

LOOKING DOWN ON THE SAN GABRIEL VALLEY.

THE ALPINE TAVERN.

or fragrant blossoms at their feet; while lovely homes are situated where the traveler would expect to find nothing but desolate crags and savage wildness. The truth is, the inhabitants have come to trust these mountains, as gentle animals sometimes learn by experience to approach man fearlessly; and, seeing what the snow-capped peaks can do for them in tempering the summer heat and furnishing them water from unfailing reservoirs, men have discerned behind their stern severity the smile of friendship and benevolence, and have perceived that these sublime dispensers of the gifts of Nature are in reality beneficent deities, — their feet upon the land which they make fertile, their hands uplifted to receive from the celestial treasure-house the blessings they in turn give freely to the grateful earth.

THE GREAT INCLINE.

To reach their serrated crests the trolley car, already mentioned, conveys us through a wild gorge known as Rubio Cañon, and leaves us at the foot of an elevated cable-road to ascend Mount Lowe. Even those familiar with the Mount

Washington and Catskill railways, or who have ascended in a similar manner to Mürren from the Vale of Lauterbrunnen, or to the summit of Mount Pilate from Lucerne, look with some trepidation at this incline, the steepest part of which has a slope of sixty-two degrees, and, audaciously, stretches into the air to a point three thousand feet above our heads. Once safely out of the cable car, however, at the upper terminus, we smile, and think the worst is over. It is

THE CIRCULAR BRIDGE.

true, we see awaiting us another innocent looking electric car by which we are to go still higher; but we are confident that nothing very terrible can be experienced in a trolley. This confidence is quickly shattered. I doubt if there is anything in the world more "hair lifting" than the road over which that car conveys its startled occupants. Its very simplicity makes it the more horrifying; for, since the vehicle is light, no massive supports are deemed essential; and, as the car is

IMITATING A BIRD.

open, the passengers seem to be traveling in a flying machine. I never realized what it was to be a bird, till I was lightly swung around a curve beneath which yawned a precipice twenty-five hundred feet in depth, or crossed a chasm by a bridge which looked in the distance like a thread of gossamer, or saw that I was riding on a scaffolding, built out from the mountain into space. For five appalling miles of alternating happiness and horror, ecstasy and dread, we twisted round the well-nigh perpendicular cliffs, until, at last the agony over, we walked into the mountain tavern near the summit, and, seating ourselves before an open fire blazing in the hall, requested some restorative nerve-food. Yet this aërial inn is only one hundred and eighty minutes from Los Angeles; and it is said that men have snowballed one another at this tavern, picked oranges at the base of the mountain, and bathed in the bay of Santa Monica, thirty miles distant, all in a single afternoon. It certainly is possible to do

SWINGING ROUND A CURVE.

this, but it should be remembered that stories are almost the only things in California which do not need irrigation to grow luxuriantly. I was told that although this mountain railway earns its running expenses it pays no interest on its enormous cost. This can readily be believed; and one marvels, not only that it was ever built, but that it was not necessary to go to a lunatic asylum for the first passenger. Nevertheless, it is a wonderfully daring experiment, and accomplishes perfectly what it was designed to do; while in proportion as one's nervousness wears away, the experience is delightful.

THE INNOCENT TROLLEY.

Living proofs of the progress made in California are the patient burros, which, previous to the construction of this railroad, formed the principal means of transportation up Mount Lowe. Why has the donkey never found a eulogist? The horse is universally admired. The Arab poet sings of the beauties of his camel. The bull, the cow, the dog, and even the cat have all been praised in prose or verse; but the poor donkey still remains an ass, the butt of ridicule, the symbol of stupidity, the object of abuse. Yet if there be another and a better world for animals, and if in that sphere patience ranks as a cardinal virtue, the ass will have a better pasture-ground than

MIDWINTER IN CALIFORNIA.

A CALIFORNIAN BURRO.

many of its rivals. The donkey's small size is against it. Most people are cruel toward dumb beasts, and only when animals have power to defend themselves, does caution make man kinder. He hesitates to hurt an elephant, and even respects, to some extent, the rear extremities of a mule; but the donkey corresponds to the small boy in a crowd of brutal playmates. It is difficult to see how these useful animals could be replaced in certain countries of the world. Purchased cheaply, reared inexpensively, living on thistles if they get nothing better, and bearing heavy burdens till they drop from exhaustion, these little beasts are of incalculable value to the laboring classes of southern Europe, Egypt, Mexico, and similar lands. If they have failed to win affection, it is, perhaps, because of their one infirmity, — their fearful vocal tones, which in America have won for them the sarcastic title of "Rocky Mountain Canaries."

ROMEO AND JULIET.

Westward from Los Angeles stretches the fa-

SAN GABRIEL VALLEY.

mous "kite-shaped" track which takes the traveler through the most celebrated orange and lemon districts of the State. Starting upon this memorable excursion, our route lay through the world-renowned San Gabriel Valley, a glorious expanse ten miles in width and seventy in length, steeped in sunshine, brilliant with every shade of yellow, emerald, and brown, and here and there enriched by spots of brighter color where beds of wild flowers swung their sweet bells noiselessly, or the light green of orange trees, with mounds of golden fruit heaped in profusion on the ground, relieved the sombre groves of eucalyptus whose foliage was so dark as to be nearly black. Occasionally, however, our train traversed a parched area which illustrated how the cloven-foot of the adversary always shows itself in spots unhallowed by the benison of water. In winter and spring, these sterile points would not be so conspicuous, but on that summer day, in spite of the closed windows, dust sometimes filled the cars, and for a little while San Gabriel Valley was a paradise lost. For seventy miles contrasts of hot sand and verdant orchards, arid wastes and smiling valley, followed one another in quick succession, — and down upon it all frowned the long wall of the Sierra Madre.

It is a wonderful experience to ride for such a distance in a perfectly level valley, and see an uninterrupted range of mountains, eight thousand feet in height, rising abruptly from the plain like the long battle-line of an invading army. What adds to its impressiveness is the fact that these peaks are, for the entire country which they dominate, the arbiters of life and death. Beyond them, on one side, the desert stretches eastward for a thousand miles; upon the other, toward the ocean, whose moisture they receive and faithfully distribute, extends this valley of delight. The height of the huge granite wall is generally uniform, save where, like towers on the mighty rampart, old San Antonio and the San Bernardino Brothers lift their hoary

GATHERING POPPIES AT THE BASE OF THE SIERRA MADRE.

AN ADOBE HOUSE.

heads two miles above the sea, — their silvery crowns and dazzling features standing out in the crystalline clearness of the atmosphere as if they had been carved in high relief.

We sped along, with feelings alternating between elation and dejection, as the scenery was beautiful or barren, till, suddenly, some sixty miles from Los Angeles, our train drew up before a city, containing asphalt pavements, buildings made of brick, and streets embowered in palms. This city which, in 1872, was a sheep-ranch, yet whose present assessed valuation is more than nine million dollars, is called Riverside; but, save in the rainy season, one looks in vain for the stream

A PASADENA LEMON TREE.

A HOUSE MODELED AFTER THE OLD MEXICAN FASHION.

from which it takes its name. The river has retired, as so many western rivers do, to wander in obscurity six feet below the sand. "A providential thing," said a wag to me, "for, in such heat as this, if the water rose to the surface it would all evaporate." The sun was, indeed, ardent as we walked through the town, and we were impressed by the fact that the dwellings most appropriate for this region are those which its first settlers seem to have instinctively adopted; for the white, one-storied adobe house, refreshing to the eye,

THE IDEAL HOME.

cool in the heat, warm in the cold, caressed by clinging vines and overhung with trees, is surely the ideal residence for Southern California. Such buildings can, of course, be greatly varied and embellished by wealthy owners; but modern houses of red brick, fanciful "Queen Annes," and imitations of castles, seem less suited to this land of sun and sand, where nothing is so much to be desired as repose in form and color. I always welcomed, therefore, genuine southern dwellings and, in the place of asphalt pavements, natural roadways domed by arching trees.

The pride of Riverside is its far-famed Magnolia Avenue, fifteen miles in length, with two broad driveways lined with pepper and eucalyptus trees. Beyond these also are palm-girt sidewalks twenty feet in breadth; while, here and there, reflecting California's golden sunshine from their glistening leaves, stand groups of the magnificent magnolias which give the avenue its name.

"Why did you make this splendid promenade?" I asked in mingled curiosity and admiration.

"It is one of our ways of booming things," was the reply; "out of the hundreds of people who come to see it, some stay, build houses, and go into business. Without it they might never have come at all."

"Was not the cost of laying it out enormous?" I inquired.

"Not so great as you would naturally suppose," was the answer, "for after this country has once been irrigated, whatever is planted on watered land will grow like interest, day and night, summer and winter."

MAGNOLIA AVENUE, RIVERSIDE.

Riverside's fortunes were made in orange culture, and there was a time when every one who planted orange trees was prosperous; but now, under inevitable competition, this enterprise is rivaled in value by other large industries, particularly the cultivation of lemons and olives. Thousands of acres of olive orchards are now flourishing in Southern California, and are considered a sure and profitable investment.

A MAGNOLIA BLOSSOM.

Another celebrated "orange city" is Redlands, where the visitor ceases to wonder at nature, and devotes himself to marveling at man. How can he do otherwise when, in a place that was a wilderness ten years ago, he drives for twenty miles over well-curbed roads, sixty feet wide and as hard as asphalt, or strolls through handsome streets adorned with palms and orange trees, and frequently embellished with residences worthy of

Newport? No doubt it is a surprise to many tourists to find such elegant homes in these cities which were born but yesterday; for Americans in the East, though far from conservative themselves, do not, as a rule, appreciate the wonderful growth of these towns which but a few years since had no existence. Occasionally some neighbor goes out to the Pacific coast, and tells his friends on his return what he has seen; but it makes little impression until they go themselves. They think he is exaggerating.

PART OF THE "CONVERTED MOUNTAIN," REDLANDS.

"Would you like to see a converted mountain?" inquired my guide.

"What do you mean?" I asked incredulously.

"You will see," he replied, "and in ten minutes we shall be there."

Accordingly, up we drove over magnificent, finely graded roads, till we arrived at what appeared to be a gentleman's private park. The park, however, seemed to have no limit, and we rode on through a bewildering extent of cemented stone walls, umbrageous trees, luxuriant flowers, trailing vines, and waving palms. At last we reached the summit, and what a view unrolled itself before us! Directly opposite, the awful wall of the Sierra swept up to meet our vision in all its majesty of granite glory, like an immense, white-crested wave, one hundred miles in length, which had by some mysterious force been instantaneously curbed and petrified, just as it was about to break and

A DRIVEWAY IN REDLANDS.

overwhelm the valley with destruction. Beneath it, for seventy miles in exquisitely blended hues, stretched the wonderful San Gabriel intervale, ideal in its tranquil loveliness. Oh, the splendor, opulence, and sweetness of its countless flowers, whose scarlet, gold, and crimson glowed and melted into the richest sheen of velvet, and rendered miles of pure air redolent with perfume, as grapes impart their flavor to good wine!

In gazing on this valley from a distance one would fain believe it to be in reality, as in appearance, an idyllic garden of Arcadian innocence and happiness, and, forgetting the disillusions of maturer years, dream that all human hearts are as transparent as its atmosphere, and that all life is no less sweet and pure.

But, presently, I asked again, "What do you mean by a *converted* mountain?"

"Eight years ago," was the reply, "this elevation on which

THE SIERRA MADRE AND THE SAN GABRIEL VALLEY.

we stand was a heap of yellow sand, like many unconverted mountains that we see about us; now it has been transformed into a dozen miles of finished roads and extensive gardens enclosing two fine residences."

"Pardon me," I exclaimed, "here are trees thirty feet high."

"All grown in eight years," he answered.

"Still," I again protested, "here are stone walls, and curbed and graded roads."

"All made in eight years," he reiterated.

"But, in addition to this mountain, how about the twenty miles of orange groves surrounding it, the thirty thousand dollar public library of Redlands, and its miles of asphalt streets?"

"All in eight years," he said again, as if, like Poe's raven, he had been taught one refrain.

In fact, it should be said that this entire mountain was purchased by two wealthy brothers who now come every winter

A FEW "UNCONVERTED MOUNTAINS," NEAR REDLANDS.

GROUNDS OF THE SMILEY BROTHERS ON THE "CONVERTED MOUNTAIN."

from the East to this incomparable hill, the whole of which has been, as if by magic, metamorphosed into an estate, where visitors are allowed to find instruction and delight upon its lofty terraces of forest and of flowers. Is it strange, then, that such sudden transformations of sterile plains and mountains into bits of paradise make tourists in Southern California wildly enthusiastic? They actually see fulfilled before their eyes the prophecy of Isaiah, "The desert shall rejoice, and blossom as the rose." The explanation is, however, simple. The land is really rich. The ingredients are already here. Instead of being worthless, as was once supposed, this is a precious soil. The Aladdin's wand that unlocks all its treasures is the irrigating ditch; its "open sesame" is water; and the divinity who, at the call of man, bestows the priceless gift, is the Madre of the Sierras. A Roman conqueror once said that he had but to stamp upon the earth and legions would spring up to do his bidding. So Capi-

IRRIGATING DITCHES.

tal has stamped upon this sandy wilderness, and in a single generation a civilized community has leaped into astonished life. Yet do we realize the immense amount of labor necessitated by such irrigation? This mountain, for example, is covered with water pipes, as electric wires are carried through our houses. Every few rods a pipe with a faucet rises from the ground; and as there are miles of roads and hundreds of cultivated acres, it can with difficulty be imagined how many of these pipes have been laid, and how innumerable are the little ditches, through which the water is made to flow. Should man relax his diligence for a single year, the region would relapse into sterility; but, on the other hand, what a land is this for those who have the skill and industry to call forth all its capabilities! What powers of productiveness may still be sleeping underneath its soil, awaiting but the kiss of water and the touch of man to waken them to life! Beside its hidden rivers what future cities may spring forth to joyous being; and what new, undiscovered chemistry may not this mingling of mountain, sun, and ocean yet evolve to prove a permanent blessing to mankind!

One hundred and twenty-six miles southwest of Los Angeles, one could imagine that he had reached the limit of the civilized world: eastward, the desert stretches far away to the bases of the San Jacinto Mountains; westward, thousands of miles of ocean billows shoulder one another toward the setting sun; southward, extends that barren, almost unknown strip of earth, the peninsula of Lower California; yet in this *cul-de-sac*, this corner between mountain, desert, and sea, rises a charming and inspiring picture, — San Diego.

The beautiful harbor of this city is almost closed, on one side, by a bold majestic promontory called Point Loma; and on the other, by a natural breakwater, in the form of a crescent, twelve miles long, upon the outer rim of which the ocean beats a ceaseless monody. At one extremity of this silver strand, directly opposite Point Loma and close to the rhythmic surf, stands the Hotel Coronado; its west front facing

SAN DIEGO.

POINT LOMA.

the Pacific, its east side looking on the azure of the peaceful bay, beyond which rises San Diego with a population of twenty thousand souls. To reach this hotel, the tourist crosses the harbor from the city by a ferry, and then in an electric car is whirled for a mile along an avenue which he might well suppose was leading him to some magnificent family estate. The pavement is delightfully smooth and hard; on

HOTEL CORONADO.

either side are waving palms and beds of radiant flowers; two charming parks, with rare botanical shrubs and trees, are, also, visible and hold invitingly before him the prospect of delightful hours in their fragrant labyrinths; and, finally, out of a semi-tropical garden, the vast extent of which he does not comprehend at first, rises the far-famed hostelry which, itself, covers about four and a half acres of ground, at the extreme southwestern corner of the Union, and on a spot which yesterday was a mere tongue of sand. In the tourist season this palatial place of entertainment presents a brilliant throng of joyous guests who have, apparently, subscribed to the motto: "All care abandon ye, who enter here." It is one of the few spots on this continent where the great faults of our American civilization — worry and incessant work — are not conspicuous. Men of the North too frequently forget that the object of life is not work, but that the object of work is life. In lands like Southern California, however, where flowers fill the air with fragrance, where fruits are so abundant that starvation is impossible, and where the

COURTYARD OF THE HOTEL.

nerves are not continually whipped by atmospheric changes into restless energy, men live more calmly, probably more rationally. Sunshine, roses, and the throbbing tones of the guitar would seem to be the most appropriate sources of amusement here. Meanwhile the northern millionaire breaks down from overwork and leaves his money to be squandered by his relatives. Yet he also, till the last gasp, claims that he is happy. What is happiness? *Quien sabe?*

The country about San Diego is a miniature reproduction of the plains of Arizona and New Mexico, and just above the city rises a genuine *mesa*, which, though comparatively small, resembles the large table-lands of the interior, and was formed in the same way. Cutting it, here and there, are little cañons, like that through which the Colorado rolls, not a mile deep, but still illustrative of the erosion made here by the rivers of a distant age; for these gashes are the result of rushing water, and every stone upon this small plateau has been worn round and smooth by friction with its fellows, tossed, whirled, and beaten by the waves of centuries.

VIEW FROM THE TABLE-LAND.

PACHANGO INDIANS AT HOME.

A CHRISTIANIZED INDIAN.

Strange, is it not, that though, like many other areas of our continent, this region was once fashioned and completely ruled by water, at present it has practically none; and men must often bring the precious liquid fifty miles to crown the soil with beauty and fertility.

The old town of San Diego, four miles north of the present city, is now almost abandoned. Only a dozen adobe buildings kept in fair repair, and as many more in ruins, mark the site. The little chapel is still used for worship, and from an uncouth wooden frame outside its walls hang two of the old Mission bells which formerly rang out the Angelus over the sunset waves. My guide carelessly struck them with the butt of his whip, and called forth from their consecrated lips of bronze a sound which, in that scene of loneliness, at first seemed like a wail of protest at the sacrilege, and finally died away into a muffled intonation resembling a stifled sob. Roused by the unexpected call,

THE MISSION BELLS.

AN AGÈD SQUAW.

there presently appeared an Indian who looked as if he might have been contemporary with Methuselah. No wrinkled leaf that had been blown about the earth for centuries could have appeared more dry and withered than this centenarian, whose hair drooped from his skull like Spanish moss, and whose brown hands resembled lumps of adobe.

"I am glad to have you see this man," said the guide, "for he has rung these bells for seventy years, and is said to be more than a hundred years old."

RELICS OF AN ANCIENT RACE.

I could not obtain a portrait of this decrepit bell-ringer, for many Indians are superstitiously opposed to being photographed; but I procured the picture of an equally shriveled female agèd one hundred and thirty who might have been his sister.

"This," remarked my guide with a smile, "is what the climate of San Diego does for the natives."

"The glorious climate of California" has been for years a theme of song and story, and a discussion of its merits forms one of the principal occupations of the dwellers on the Pacific coast. It is indeed difficult to see how tourists could pass their time here without this topic of conversation, so infinite is its variety and so debatable are many of the conclusions drawn from it. It is the Sphinx of California; differing, however, from the Sphinx of Egypt in that it offers a new problem every day. The literature that treats of the Pacific coast fairly bristles with statistics on this subject, and many writers have found it impossible to resist the temptation of adorning their pages with tables of humidity, temperature, and rainfall. Some hotels even print in red letters at the top of the stationery furnished to their guests:

"The temperature to-day is ——."

Among the photographs of San Diego are several which represent groups of ecstatic bathers, ranging from small boys to elderly bald-headed gentlemen, apparently ready to take a plunge into the Pacific; while beneath them is displayed the legend, "January 1, 18—." Candor compels me, however, to

"ECSTATIC BATHERS."

MIDWINTER AT LOS ANGELES.

state that, as far as I was able to ascertain, these pictured bathers rarely pay a New Year's call to Neptune in his mighty palace, but content themselves in winter with going no further than his ante-chambers, — the sheltered, sun-warmed areas of public bath-houses.

"I believe this to be the best climate in the world," said a gentleman to me in San Diego, "but I confess that, when strangers are visiting me, it occasionally does something it ought not to do."

The truth is, there are several climates in Southern California, some of which are forced upon the resident, while others can be secured by going in search of them in a trolley car or a railway carriage. The three determining factors in the problem of temperature are the desert, the ocean, and the mountains. Thus, in midsummer, although it may be fiercely hot in the inland valleys, it is invariably cool in the mountains on account of their altitude, and near the shore because the hot air rising from the desert invites a daily ocean breeze. Even at a distance from the comfortable coast, humanity never passes into that abject, panting, and perspiring condition in which the inhabitants of the Eastern States are usually seen when the mercury goes to ninety. The nights are always cool; although not quite as much so in July as the enthusiasts tell us who have never seen the country later in the season than the month of May, and who weary us with the threadbare tale of never sleeping without a blanket.

"Is it true, madam," I said to a lady of San Diego, "that here one must always take a blanket to bed with him?"

"Hush," she replied, "never ask that question unless you are sure that there are no tourists within hearing."

PIER AT SANTA MONICA.

AVALON, SANTA CATALINA ISLAND.

Three statements are, I think, unquestionably accurate: first, that for many months of the year the residents need not take into consideration for a moment the possibility of rain; second, that on account of this drought there must inevitably be during that period a superfluity of dust; and, third, that every day there will be felt "a cool refreshing breeze," which frequently increases to a strong wind. My memory of California will always retain a vivid impression of this wind, and the effect of it upon the trees is evident from the fact that it has compelled most of them to lean toward the east, while one of the last sights I beheld in San Diego was a man chasing his hat. Nevertheless, acclimated Californians would no more complain of their daily breeze, however vigorous, than a man would speak disrespectfully of his mother.

As in most semi-tropical countries, there is a noticeable difference in temperature between sun and shade. In the sun one feels a genial glow, or even a decided heat; but let him step into the shade, or stand on a street-corner waiting for a car, and the cool wind from the mountains or the ocean will be felt immediately. People accustomed to these changes pay little heed to them; but to new-comers the temperature of the shade, and even that of the interiors of the hotels and houses, appears decidedly cool.

One day, in June, I was invited to dine at a fruit-ranch a few miles from Pasadena. The heat in the sun was intense, and I noticed that the mercury indicated ninety-five degrees; but, unlike the atmosphere of New York in a heated term, the air did not remind me of a Turkish bath. The heat of Southern California is dry, and it is absolutely true that the highest temperature of an arid region rarely entails as much physical discomfort as a temperature fifteen or twenty degrees lower in the Eastern States, when accompanied by humidity. The moisture in a torrid atmosphere is what occasions most of the distress and danger, the best proof of which is the fact that while, every summer, hundreds of people are prostrated by sunstroke near the Atlantic coast, such a calamity has never occurred in New

NOT AFRAID OF THE SUN.

Mexico, Arizona, or California. Moreover, when the mercury in Los Angeles rises, as it occasionally does, to one hundred degrees, the inhabitants of that city have a choice of several places of refuge: in two or three hours they can reach the mountains; or in an hour they can enjoy themselves upon Redondo Beach; or they may take a trolley car and, sixty minutes later, stroll along the sands of Santa Monica, inhaling a refreshing breeze, blowing practically straight from Japan; or, if none of these resorts is sufficiently attractive, three hours after leaving Los Angeles they can fish on Santa Catalina Island, a little off the coast; or linger in the groves of Santa Barbara; or, perhaps, best of all can be invigorated by the saline breath of the Pacific sweeping through the corridors of the Coronado. Santa Catalina Island is, in particular, a delightful pleasure-resort, whose beautiful, transparent waters, remarkable fishing-grounds, and soft,

IN COTTONWOOD CAÑON, SANTA CATALINA.

LILIPUTIAN AND GIANT.

though tonic-giving air, which comes to it from every point of the compass over a semi-tropic sea, are so alluring that thousands of contented people often overflow its hotels and camp in tents along the beach.

That the winter climate of Southern California, not only on the coast, but in the interior, is delightful, is beyond ques-

ON THE BEACH AT SANTA CATALINA.

tion. What was healthful a hundred years ago to the Spanish monks who settled here, proved equally so to those adventurous "Forty-niners" who entered California seeking gold, and is still more beneficial to those who now come to enjoy its luxuries and comforts. Flowers and fruit are found here throughout the entire year. The rainy days are few, and frosts are as ephemeral as the dew; and to the agèd, the invalids, the fugitives from frost, and the "fallen soldiers of civilization," who are no longer able to make a courageous fight with

AN OLD CALIFORNIAN TRADING POST.

eastern storms and northern cold, San Diego is a climatic paradise. Accordingly, from early October until April the overland trains roll westward from a land of snow and frost to one of sun and flowers, bearing an annually increasing multitude of invalids and pleasure-seekers, some of whom have expensive permanent homes and costly ranches here — like that of Mr. Andrew McNally, at Altadena—while others find abundant comfort in the fine hotels.

A BIT OF NATURE ON THE COAST.

Perhaps the principal secret of the charm of the winter climate of Southern California, as well as that of its wonderful health-restoring properties, lies in the fact that its dry, pure air and even temperature make it possible for one to live continuously out of doors. Yet, though not cold, it is a temperature cool enough to be free from summer languor.

CALIFORNIAN PALMS.

Especially attractive to the visitors from the North are the palms of Southern California. Many of these resemble monstrous pineapples terminating in gigantic ferns. What infinite variety the palm tree has, now dwarfed in height, yet sending out on every side a mass of thick green leaves; now rising straight as an obelisk from the desert sand, and etching its fine feathery tufts against the sky; now bearing luscious fruit of different kinds; now furnishing material for clothing, fishing-nets, and matting; or putting forth those slender fronds, frequently twenty feet in length, which are sent North by florists to decorate dwellings and churches for festivals and weddings! The palm is typical of the South, as the pine is of the North. One hints to us of brilliant skies, a tropic sun, and an easy, indolent existence; the other suggests bleak mountains and the forests of northern hills, and symbolizes the conflict there between man and nature, in which both fortitude and daring have been needful to make man the conqueror. One finds a fascination in contrasting these two children of old Mother Earth, and thinks of Heine's lines:

"A pine tree standeth lonely
On a northern mountain's height;
It sleeps, while around it is folded
A mantle of snowy white.

It is dreaming of a palm tree
In a far-off Orient land,
Which lonely and silent waiteth
In the desert's burning sand."

On my last day at San Diego, I walked in the morning sunshine on Coronado Beach. The beauty of the sea and shore was almost indescribable: on one side rose Point Loma, grim and gloomy as a fortress wall; before me

HERMIT VALLEY NEAR SAN DIEGO.

THE PACIFIC.

stretched away to the horizon the ocean with its miles of breakers curling into foam; between the surf and the city, wrapped in its dark blue mantle, lay the sleeping bay; eastward, the mingled yellow, red, and white of San Diego's buildings glistened in the sunlight like a bed of coleus; beyond the city heaved the rolling plains, rich in their garb of golden brown, from which rose distant mountains, tier on tier, wearing the purple veil which Nature here loves oftenest to weave for them; while, in the foreground, like a jewel in a brilliant setting, stood the Coronado.

The fascination of Southern California had at last completely captured me. Its combination of ocean, desert, and mountain, its pageantry of color, and its composite life of city, ranch, and beach had cast over me a magic spell. It was, however, a lonely sea that spread its net of foam before my feet. During my stay I had not seen a single steamer on

"A SEA-BIRD FASHIONED BY MAN'S HAND."

its surface, and only rarely had a few swift sea-birds, fashioned by man's hand, dotted the azure for a little with their white wings, ere they dipped below the horizon's rim. Hence, though the old, exhilarating, briny odor was the same, I felt that, as an ocean, this was unfamiliar. The Atlantic's waves are haunted by historic memories, but few reminders of antiquity rise ghostlike from the dreary waste of the Pacific. Few battles have been fought, few conquests made upon these shores. On the Atlantic coast one feels that he is looking off toward civilized and friendly lands, across a sea which ocean greyhounds have made narrow; but here three purple islands, floating on the limitless expanse, suggest mysterious archipelagoes scattered starlike on its area, thousands of miles away, before a continent is reached; and one vaguely imagines unknown races, coral reefs, and shores of fronded palms, where Nature smiles indulgently upon a pagan paradise. Nevertheless its very mystery and vastness give to the Pacific a peculiar charm, which changeful Orient seas, and even the turbulent Atlantic, never can impart. Instinctively we stand uncovered in the presence of the mightiest ocean on our planet. It is at once the symbol and the fact of majesty; and the appalling sense of trackless space which it inspires, the rhythm of unmeasured and immeasureable waves, together with the moaning of the surf upon the sand, at times completely overwhelm us with suggestions of the Infinite, until no language seems appropriate, unless it shapes itself in prayer.

In Helen Hunt Jackson's novel, "Ramona," the romance of this region has found immortality. What "Romola" is to

A LONELY OCEAN.

RAMONA'S HOME.

mediæval Florence, "Ramona" is to Southern California. It has embalmed in the memory of the nation a lost cause and a vanished race. Less than one hundred years ago, where the Anglo-Saxon has since built railroads, erected manufactories, and created cities, a life was lived, so different in its character from all that followed or preceded it, that only a story like

THE CHAPEL, RAMONA'S HOME.

"Ramona" could make it appear real. At that time about twenty "Missions"—which were in reality immense ecclesiastical farms—bordered the coast for seven hundred miles. For when the New World had been suddenly revealed to the astonished gaze of Europe, it was not merely the adventurous conqueror who hastened to these shores. The priest accompanied him, and many enthusiastic soldiers of the Cross embarked to bear to the benighted souls beyond the sea the tidings of salvation. Missionary enterprises were not then what they are today. Nothing was known with certainty of the strange tribes on this side of the globe, and there was often a heroism in the labors of self-sacrificing missionaries to America, which far surpassed the courage of the buccaneer. Many exploring expeditions to this western land received the blessing of the Church, and were conducted, not alone for obtaining territory and gold, but for the conversion of

PALMS NEAR SAN FERNANDO MISSION.

the inhabitants. In Mexico and Peru the priests had followed, rather than led the way; but in California, under the lead of Father Junipero, they took the initiative, and the salvation of souls was one of the principal purposes of the invaders. This did not, however, prevent the Franciscans, who took possession of the land, from selecting with great wisdom its very best locations; but, having done so, they soon brought tens of thousands of Indians under spiritual and temporal control. These natives were, for the most part, as gentle and teachable as the Fathers were patient and wise; and, in 1834, a line of Missions stretched from San Diego to Monterey, and the converted Indians numbered about twenty thousand, many of whom had been trained to be carpenters, masons, blacksmiths, saddlers, tailors, millers, and farmers. Three-quarters of a million cattle grazed upon the Mission pastures, as well as sixty thousand horses; fruits, grain, and flowers grew in their well-cultivated valleys until the country blossomed like the Garden of the Lord; and in the midst of all this industry and agricultural prosperity the native converts obeyed their Christian masters peacefully and happily, and came as near to a state of civilization as Indians have ever come.

CORRIDOR, SAN FERNANDO MISSION.

Presently the Mexicans made their appearance here; but, though they held and managed enormous ranches, the situa-

SANTA BARBARA.

tion was comparatively unchanged; for they maintained harmonious relations with the Missions, and had no serious difficulties with the Indians. Thus life went on for nearly half a century, and seemed to the good Fathers likely to go on forever; for who, they thought, would ever cross the awful eastern plains to interfere with their Arcadian existence, or what invading force would ever approach them over the lonely sea? But history repeats itself. The Missions soon became too rich not to excite cupidity; and those who coveted

SAN JUAN CAPISTRANO.

their lands and herds declared, as an excuse for violence, that the poor Indians were held in a state of slavery, and should be made to depend upon themselves. At length, in 1833, the Mexican Government by a decree of secularization ruined the Missions; but the Indians, although not so prosperous and well treated as under the Fathers, still kept, through Mexican protection, most of their privileges and the lands they owned. Finally came the Anglo-Saxon, and, under the imperious civilization that poured into California from 1840 to 1860, the pastoral age soon disappeared. The Missions, which had already lost much of their property and power under the

Mexican Government, quickly shrank after this new invasion into decrepitude. The practical Anglo-Saxon introduced railroads, electricity, commerce, mammoth hotels, and scientific irrigation, all of which the Fathers, Mexicans, and Indians never would have cared for. Nevertheless, with his arrival, the curtain fell upon as peaceful a life-drama as the world had seen.

To the reader, thinker, and poet the memories and associations of these Missions form, next to the gifts of Nature,

GROUP OF FRANCISCAN FRIARS.

the greatest charm of Southern California; and, happily, although that semi-patriarchal life has passed away, its influence still lingers; for, scattered along the coast — some struggling in poverty, some lying in neglect — are the adobe churches, cloisters, and fertile Mission-fields of San Juan Capistrano, San Fernando Rey, Santa Monica, Santa Barbara, and Santa Cruz, all of which still preserve the soft and gracious names, so generously given in those early days, and fill us with a genuine reverence for the sandaled monks, who by incessant toil transformed this barren region into a garden, covered these boundless plains with flocks and herds, and dealt

CHIEF OF A TRIBE OF MISSION INDIANS.

so wisely with the Indians that even their poor descendants, to-day, reverence their memory.

The Saxon has done vastly more, it is true; but, in some ways, he has done much less. The very names which he bequeathed to places not previously christened by the Spaniards, such as Gold Gulch, Hell's Bottom, and Copperopolis, tell a more forcible, though not as beautiful a tale, as the melodious titles, San Buenaventura, San Francisco Dolores, Santa Clara, San Gabriel, and La Purissima.

It is not, therefore, the busy streets and handsome dwellings of Los Angeles and Pasadena, but the adobe ruins, the battered statues, the cracked and voiceless bells, the poor remnants of the Indian tribes, and even the old Spanish names, behind which lies a century of sanctity and romance, which give to Southern California an atmosphere of the Old World and harmonize most perfectly with its history.

INDIAN WOMEN.

SAN DIEGO MISSION.

Most of the Mission buildings are in a sad condition. Earthquakes have shattered some; neglect and malice have disfigured others; but a society, composed alike of Catholics and Protestants, is now, in the interest of the past, endeavoring to rescue them from utter ruin. It is a worthy task. What subjects for a painter most of them present! How picturesque are their old cloisters, looming up dark, grand, and desolate against the sky! How worn and battered are they by the storms of years! How tremblingly stands the Cross upon their ancient towers, as if its sacred form had become feeble like the fraternity that once flourished here! What witnesses they are of an irrevocable past! Their crumbling walls, if they could speak, might grow sublimely eloquent, and thrill us with inspiring tales of heroism, patience, tact, and fortitude exhibited when these Missions bloomed like flowery oases on the arid areas of the South and West, and taught a faith of which their melancholy cloisters are the sad memorials.

Ten miles from Los Angeles, the Southern Pacific railroad passes a long edifice, the massive walls of which might lead us to suppose it was a fortress, but for its cross and a few antiquated bells. It is the church of the San Gabriel Mission. All other buildings of the institution have disappeared; but this old edifice remains, and, unless purposely destroyed by man, may stand here for five centuries more, since its enormous walls are five feet thick, and the mortar used in their construction has rendered them almost as solid as if hewn from rock. As I descended, at the station a quarter of a mile away, a little barefooted Mexican boy approached and shyly offered me his hand. "Are you the Father," he asked?

"No," I said, "I am not the Father, but I have come to see the church; can you show it to me?"

"But Padre Joaquin said I was to meet a Father."

"Well," I answered, "I am the only passenger who has come by this train, so you had better walk back with me."

The Mexican boys seem to be the best part of what Mexico has left in California. This lad, for example, was attending an American school, and appeared bright and ambi-

SAN GABRIEL MISSION CHURCH.

tious, though so extremely courteous and respectful that he seemed almost timid. The little hut in which he lived was opposite the church, and he seemed perfectly familiar with the sacred structure. "See," he said, pointing to some mutilated wooden statues in the poor, scantily furnished sacristy, "here are some images which cannot be used, they are so broken, and here are more," he added, opening some drawers and displaying four or five smaller figures in various stages of dilapidation. Thus, for some time he continued to call my attention to different curious relics with such interest and reverence that I was almost sorry when Father Joaquin appeared. It was sad to see the altar of the church defaced

DISCARDED SAINTS, SAN GABRIEL.

MUTILATED STATUES.

and cracked, and its statues, brought a hundred years ago from Spain, scarcely less battered than those which the boy had shown me in the sacristy. Yet it was plain that worshipers as well as vandals had been here. The basins for holy water, cut in the solid wall, were worn, like the steps of an ancient building, with countless fingers, long since turned to dust. There, also, were two old confessionals, one of which was so hopelessly infirm that it had been set aside at last, to listen to no more whispered tales of sin and sorrow. The doors of the church at first looked ancient, but wore a really modern air, when compared with the original portals, which, no longer able to stand upright, had been laid against the wall, to show to tourists. Yet, eighty years ago, this church stood proudly at the head of all the Missions, and reared its cross above the richest of their valleys. According to Father Joaquin's estimate, the Fathers of San Gabriel must have had twenty thousand acres under cultivation, and, in 1820, this Mission alone possessed one hundred and sixty thousand vines, two thousand three hundred trees, twenty-five thousand head of cattle, and fifteen thousand sheep. "It was all ours," he said, with a sweep of his hand, "we had reclaimed it from the desert, and, by the treaty between the United States and Mexico, we were allowed to retain all lands that we had cultivated. Yet

THE BAPTISMAL FONT.

of those twenty thousand acres, one hundred and fifty are all that are left us!"

The Padre accompanied me to the station. "How large is your parish, Father?" I asked.

"It is thirteen miles long," was his reply, "and I have in it eight hundred souls, but most of them live too far away to walk to church, and are too poor to ride."

"And how many Indians have you?"

SAN GABRIEL, FROM THE SOUTHEAST.

"Perhaps a hundred," he answered, "and even they are dying off."

"What of their character?" I asked.

"They have sadly fallen away," was the response. "True, they are Christians as far as they are anything, but they are hopelessly degraded, yet they respect the Church, and are obedient and reverential when under its influence."

Most of the Californian Missions are really dead, and near that of La Purissima may still be seen the rent in the ground made by the earthquake which destroyed it. Others, like San Gabriel and San Juan Capistrano, are dragging out a moribund

A DEGENERATE.

existence, under the care of only one or two priests, who move like melancholy phantoms through the lonely cloisters, and pray among the ruins of a noble past. The Mission of Santa Barbara, however, is in fairly good repair, and a few Franciscan Fathers still reside there and carry on a feeble imitation of their former life.

It is on his way to this Mission that the traveler passes the reputed residence of Ramona. There is, it is true, another structure near San Diego which, also, claims this distinction; but the ranch on the route from Los Angeles to Santa Barbara perfectly corresponds to "H. H.'s" descriptions of her heroine's home, with its adjoining brook and willows, and hills surmounted by the cross. The house is almost hidden by the trees with which a Mexican ordinarily surrounds his dwelling, and is, as usual, only one story high, with a projecting roof, forming a porch along the entire front. As we learn in "Ramona," much of the family

THE CROSS ON THE HILL.

life in those old days — sewing, visiting, and siesta-taking — went on in the open air, under the shade of the porticos which were wide and low. Here it was that Alessandro brought Felipe back to health, watching and nursing him as he slept outdoors on his rawhide bed; and we may see the arbor where the lovers met, the willows where they were surprised by Señora Moreno, and the hills on which the pious lady caused wooden crosses to be reared, that passers-by might know that some good Catholics were still left in California.

The Mission of Santa Barbara is of solid brick and stone, with walls six feet in thickness. Its cloisters look sufficiently massive to defy an earthquake, and are paved with enormous bricks each twelve inches square. The huge red tiles of the roof, also, tell of a workmanship which, although rude, was honest and enduring. The interior, however, is of little interest, for the poor relics which the Fathers keep are even less attractive than those displayed at the Mission of San Gabriel; yet there are shown at least two enormous missals which are no less than

SANTA BARBARA MISSION.

SANTA BARBARA MISSION, FROM THE FARM.

WHERE THE FATHERS WALKED.

four feet long by two feet wide, and beautifully inscribed on parchment.

"What is the Mission's income?" I asked the gentle monk who acted as my guide.

"Alas!" he answered, "we have very little. You know our lands are gone. We have barely twenty-five acres now. Moreover, we are outside the village; and, as there is another church, most Catholics go there. We receive, indeed, occasional offerings from travelers; but we are very poor."

"Who cultivates your twenty-five acres?" I inquired.

"According to our ability, we are all busy," was the answer, "some till the garden; others train young men for the priesthood; one of our number is a carpenter; and another," he added, evidently laughing at his own expense, "knows just enough about machinery to make a bad break worse."

"And the Indians?" I said.

"Not one is left," was the reply. "Though once the Mis-

THE CEMETERY, SANTA BARBARA.

sion counted them by thousands, they are all dead and gone. There are their monuments," he added, pointing to the fragments of a mill and one or two industrial shops.

I looked and saw the remnants of a giant wheel which formerly had been turned by water, brought from the hills to feed the Fathers' lands. The water was still flowing, but the wheel lay, broken, — symbolic of the link which bound the Mission to the vanished past.

The first Roman Catholic Bishop of California and some of the early Fathers are buried in the chapel of the monastery, but interments are now made in a neighboring cemetery, strictly reserved for members of the Mission, each of whom has there his predestined place. Yet even in this humble Campo Santo life will not yield entirely to death. The hum of droning insects breaks the stillness of the empty cloisters; occasionally a lizard darts like a tongue of flame along the walls; grasses and trailing plants adorn impartially the ground containing human dust, and that which still awaits an occupant; while round a stately crucifix, which casts its shadow like a benediction on the sleeping dead, sweet wild flowers bloom throughout the year, and from their swinging censers offer incense to the figure of the Saviour with each passing breeze. The hush of melancholy broods over the entire place. The mountains, gazing down upon it in stony silence, are haggard and forbidding; below it lies the modern town; while from a neighboring hillside the inmates of a villa look directly into the monastery garden, on which the earlier Fathers little dreamed a female eye would ever rest. A little life, however, was still visible about this Santa Barbara Mission. Two brown-robed monks were hoeing in the field; occasionally, visitors came and went; and, just as I was leaving, one of the priests, in obedience to a summons,

DREAMING OF OTHER DAYS.

hurried away to minister to the sick; yet over all there hung an atmosphere of unreality and sadness. I felt myself the guest of an anachronism.

A fashionable city has risen at the feet of these old monks, but they regard it not. A trolley car brings curious tourists to their doors; but the ways of the Santa Barbara Fathers are those of long ago. Like agèd pilgrims, dreaming by their firesides, they seem to be living in the past; they certainly have no present worthy of the name; and when I sought to draw forth from my priestly guide some idea of their future, he answered me by pointing to a grave.

GRAND CAÑON OF THE COLORADO RIVER

THE SAN FRANCISCO VOLCANOES.

THE GRAND CAÑON OF THE COLORADO

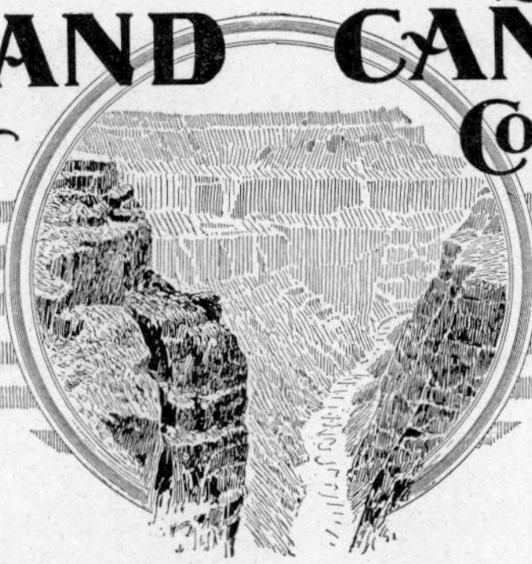

WHILE the Old World is better able than the New to satisfy the craving of the mind for art and history, no portion of our globe can equal the North American continent in certain forms of natural scenery which reach the acme of sublimity. Niagara, the Yosemite, the Yellowstone National Park, and the Grand Cañon of the Colorado in Arizona are the four great natural wonders of America. Niagara is Nature in the majesty of liquid motion, where, as the outlet of vast inland seas, a mighty river leaps in wild delirium into a gorge two hundred feet below, and boils

A PETRIFIED FOREST, ARIZONA.

and seethes tumultuously till its heart is set at rest and its fever cooled by the embrace of Lake Ontario. The Yosemite is Nature pictured, in a frame of granite precipices, as reclining on a carpet woven with a million flowers, above which rise huge trees three centuries old,

PACK-MULES OF THE DESERT.

which, nevertheless, to the spectator, gazing from the towering cliffs, appear like waving ferns. The Yellowstone Park is the arena of an amphitheatre in which fire and water, the two great forces which have made our planet what it is, still languidly contend where formerly they struggled desperately for supremacy. But the Grand Cañon of Arizona is Nature wounded unto

EVIDENCES OF EROSION.

THE NAVAJO CHURCH.

FANTASTIC FORMS.

death, and lying stiff and ghastly with a gash, two hundred miles in length and a mile in depth, in her bared breast, from which is flowing fast a stream of life-blood called the Colorado.

The section of country through which one travels to behold this last-named marvel is full of mystery and fascination. It is a land where rivers frequently run underground or cut their way through gorges of such depth that the bewildered tourist, peering over their precipitous cliffs, can hardly gain a glimpse of the streams flowing half a mile below; a land of colored landscapes such as elsewhere would be deemed impossible, with "painted deserts," red and yellow rocks, petrified forests, brown grass and purple grazing grounds; a land where from a sea of tawny sand, flecked here and there with bleached bones, like whitecaps on the ocean, one gazes upon mountains glistening with snow; and where at times the intervals are so brief between aridity and flood, that one might choose, like Alaric, a river-bed for his sepulchre, yet see a host like that of Pharaoh drowned in it before the dawn. In almost every other portion of the world

A SPECIMEN OF NATURE'S HANDIWORK.

Nature reveals her finished work; but here she partially discloses the secrets of her skill, and shows to us her modes of earth-building. Thus, the entire country is dotted with *mesas*, or table-lands of sandstone, furrowed and fashioned in a tremendous process of erosion, caused by the draining through this area of a prehistoric ocean, whose rushing, whirling, and receding waters molded the mountains, carved the cañons, and etched innumerable grotesque figures and fantastic forms. A feeling of solemnity steals over us, as we reflect upon the lapse of geologic time which such a record covers, unnumbered ages before man's advent on this planet; and these deep cañons and eroded valleys, whose present streams are only miniature representatives of those which formerly wrought havoc here, teach lessons of patience to the restless mortals who behold them; while some of the singular formations on the cliffs present perplexing problems which Nature, as it were in mocking humor, bids us solve.

Was Nature ever really sportive? In the old days, when she produced her uncouth monsters of the deep, was she in manner, as in age, a child? Did she then play with her continents, and smile to see them struggle up from the sea only to sink again? Was it caprice that made her wrap her vast dominions in the icy bands of glaciers, or pour upon them lava torrents, and frequently convulse them with a mighty earthquake? If so, New Mexico and Arizona must have been her favorite playgrounds. At many points her rock formations look like whimsical imitations of man's handicraft, or specimens of the colossal vegetation of an earlier age. Some are gigantic, while others bear a ludicrous resemblance to misshapen dwarfs, suggesting, as they stand like pygmies round their mightier brethren, a group of mediæval jesters in a court of kings. In the faint dusk of evening, as one flits by them in the moving train, their weird, uncanny forms appear to writhe in pain, and he is tempted to regard them as the material shapes of tortured souls.

The *mesas* of New Mexico and Arizona are, usually, regular in outline, sometimes resembling in the distance cloud-banks on the edge of the horizon, but oftener suggesting mighty fortresses, or ramparts to resist invasion, like the wall of China. These are not only beautiful in form and color, but from the fact that

A MESA.

they recall the works of man, we gaze at them with wonder, and find in them a fascinating interest. They prove that Nature needs some human association to appeal strongly to us, and how man's history of smiles and tears gives pathos, mystery, and romance to scenes which otherwise would be merely coldly beautiful or terribly sublime. It is for this reason, doubtless, that we are always endeavoring to personify Nature. We think of solitary trees as lonely, of storm-tossed waves as angry, and

A GROUP OF MESAS.

of a group of mountains as members of one family. Thus some of the Arizona mountains are called brothers. No doubt their birth was attended by the same throes of Mother Earth, and they possess certain family resemblances in their level summits, huge square shoulders, and the deep furrows in their rugged cheeks; while all of them evince the same disdain for decoration, scorning alike the soft rich robes of verdure and the rough storm-coats of the pines.

The idea of companionship in Nature is not wholly fanciful. Is not the fundamental law of the universe the attraction which one mass of matter has for another? Even the awful distances

ON THE OLD SANTA FÉ TRAIL.

in interstellar space form no exception to this rule; for telescopic scrutiny reveals the fact that planets, suns, and systems move in harmony, on paths which indicate that they are all associated in the stupendous drama of the skies. The human interest connected with the mountains and the *mesas* of New Mexico and Arizona is not very great. No mediæval mystery haunts these castles sculptured by the hand of Nature. No famous romancer has lighted on their cliffs the torch of his poetic

AN ARIZONA CLOUD-EFFECT.

fancy. No poet has yet peopled them with creatures of his imagination. We can, unfortunately, conjure up from their majestic background no more romantic picture than that of some Pueblo Indian wooing his dusky bride. Yet they are not without some reminiscences of heroism; for valiant men, a half century ago, following the westward moving star of empire, braved almost inconceivable hardships in their shadow, when, after four thousand years, American pioneers repeated the old, old story, begun upon the plains of Shinar, as the "Sons of the East"

OLD HOME OF KIT CARSON, TAOS, N. M.

went westward in their quest of fortune. How few of us think of those unrecorded heroes now, as we cross this region in luxurious cars! To most of us the dead, whose bones once whitened many of these lonely plains, are nothing more than the last winter's snowdrifts melted by the sun; yet how effectively the Saxon has succeeded in his conquest of the continent we have continual evidence as we glide swiftly, from the Atlantic to the Pacific, through glowing grain fields, prosperous cities, and states that rival empires in size. Where formerly the Spanish conquerors, in their fruitless search for

GRAVE OF KIT CARSON, TAOS, N. M.

the reputed Seven Cities glittering with gold, endured privations and exhibited bravery which have hardly been surpassed in the entire history of the world; and where, too, as if it were but yesterday, the American Argonauts toiled painfully for months through tribes of hostile Indians, across desert wastes and over cloud-encompassed mountains, we find ourselves the inmates of a rolling palace, propelled by one of Nature's tireless forces,

THE BRIDGE OF CAÑON DIABLO.

and feel at times in our swift flight as if we were the occupants of a cushioned cannon-ball of glass. Even the crossing of one of the many viaducts along our route is a reminder of how science has been summoned to assist the invader in his audacious enterprise of girdling a continent with steel.

The art of bridge-building in some form or other is one of the earliest necessities of civilization. Even the apes in equatorial regions will link themselves together, and swing their living line across a stream to trees on the opposite bank, thus forming a connected path of bodies along which other monkeys pass in safety. Bridges of ropes or reeds are, also, made by

HOMES OF CLIFF DWELLERS.

the most primitive of men; while viaducts of stone rose gradually in perfection, from the rude blocks heaped up by savages to the magnificent structures fashioned by the Romans. But with the introduction of iron and steel into their composition, bridges are now constructed quickly, with consummate skill, and in a multitude of different forms assist in making possible the safe and rapid transit of our great Republic.

In addition to all the wonderful natural features of Arizona and New Mexico, the insight into ancient and modern Indian life which they afford is of extraordinary interest, particularly

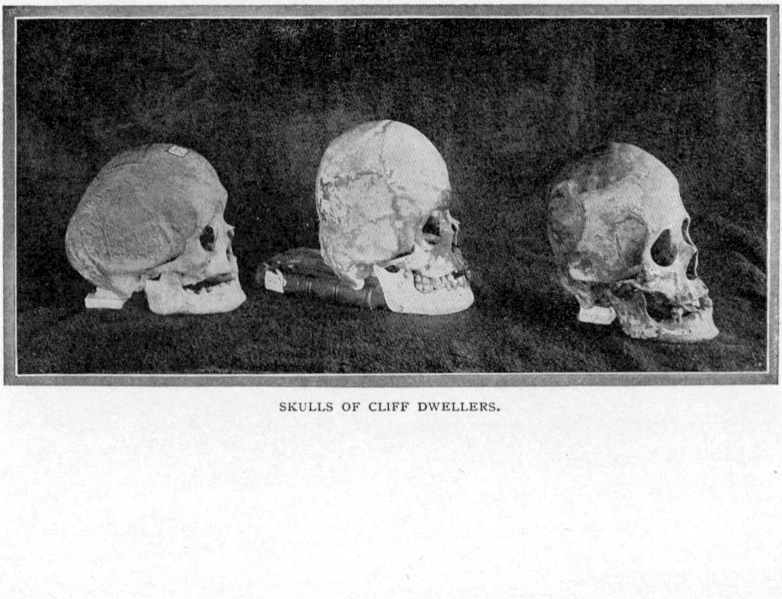

SKULLS OF CLIFF DWELLERS.

LAGUNA.

as aboriginal civilization, evidently, reached a higher level here than was attained by any of the tribes which roamed throughout the regions now known as the Middle and Eastern States. The natives of the arid regions of the great Southwest, though subdivided into numerous tribes, are usually known under the general title of Pueblos. The name itself, bestowed upon them by the Spaniards, is significant; since *pueblo* is the Spanish word for village, and this would seem to prove that the race

CLIFF PALACES.

thus designated three hundred and fifty years ago was not nomadic, but had been settled here for many years.

Antiquity and mystery impart a charm to these Pueblo Indians. They are foundlings of history. We see their immemorial settlements, and know that, centuries before Columbus landed on San Salvador, a number of advantageously situated places in the western portion of this continent served as the homes of powerful tribes, whose towns and villages formed

A TWO-STORY CLIFF PALACE.

the scenes of warfare and barbaric splendor. But of the men who built those villages we know comparatively nothing. Their origin is almost as trackless as the sand which hides so many of their relics in a tawny sepulchre. We may be certain, however, that the remnants who survive are the representatives of myriads who once made most of the American valleys palpitant with life, but over whom oblivion has swept like a huge tidal wave, leaving the scattered fragments of their history like peaks rising from a submerged world.

The best conclusions of scientists in regard to the geological periods of our planet consider that the Glacial Epoch began about two hundred and forty thousand, and ended about eighty thousand, years ago. Traces of the existence of men in North America during that glacial period have been found in abundance, and make it probable that a human population existed, toward the close of that era, all the way from the Atlantic

Coast to the Upper Mississippi Valley. Where these men of the Ice Age originally came from is a matter of conjecture; but it seems probable that they migrated hither from the Old World, since it is certain that during the various elevations and depressions of the two continents, it was possible, several times, for men to go from Europe or from Asia into America without crossing any ocean, either by the northwestern corner of Alaska, which has been repeatedly joined to Siberia through the elevation of the shallow Bering Sea, or by the great Atlantic ridge which more than once has risen above the ocean between Great Britain and Greenland. Yet, though the first inhabitants of America, in all probability, came thus from the Old World at a very distant period of antiquity, it is believed by the best students of the subject that, until within the last few centuries, there had been no intercourse between America and either Europe or Asia, for at least twenty thousand years. Hence the Aborigines of this continent developed in the course of ages peculiarities which distinguish them from other races, and justify their being regarded as, practically, native to the soil.

The Indians of New Mexico and Arizona were, probably, fugitives from more fertile lands, whence they had been expelled by the ancestors of the bloodthirsty and cruel Apaches.

AN EARLY PLACE OF SHELTER.

The country to which they came, and where they made a final stand against their predatory foes, was well adapted to defense. For hundreds of square miles the land is cleft with chasms, and dotted with peculiar, isolated table-lands hundreds of feet in height, with almost perfectly level surfaces and precipitous sides. The origin and formation of these *mesas*, due to erosion through unnumbered centuries, by water draining from an inland sea, has been already referred to, and it can be readily seen that they originally formed ideal residences for the peace-loving Pueblos, who either made their homes as Cliff Dwellers in the crevices of cañon walls, or took advantage of these lofty rocks, already shaped and fortified by Nature, and built on them their dwellings. These in themselves were no mean strongholds. Their thick walls, made of rock fragments cemented with adobe, constituted a natural fortress, against which weapons such as savages used before they acquired firearms could do little harm; and even these houses the Indians con-

"CREVICES OF CAÑON WALLS."

THE SUMMIT OF A MESA.

structed like the cliffs themselves, lofty and perpendicular, tier above tier, and, save for ladders, almost as inaccessible as eagles' nests. Again, since these *pueblos* stood on table-lands, the approach to which could be easily defended, they were almost impregnable; while their isolation and elevation, in the treeless regions of New Mexico, enabled watchmen to discover the approach of an enemy at a considerable distance and to give warning for the women, children, and cattle roaming on the plain to be brought to a place of safety. The instinct of self-preservation and even the methods of defense are, after all, almost identical in every age and clime; and the motive which led the Indians to the summits of these *mesas* was, no doubt, the same that prompted the Athenians to make a citadel of their Acropolis, and mediæval knights to build their castles on the isolated crags of Italy, or on the mountain peaks along the Rhine.

As times became more peaceful, the Pueblos located their villages upon the plains, and one of these, called Laguna, is

THE MESA ENCANTADA.

now a station of the Santa Fé railway. But a mere glance at this, in passing, was far too brief and unsatisfactory for our purpose, aside from the fact that its proximity to the railroad had, naturally, robbed the settlement of much of its distinctive character. We therefore resolved to leave our train, and go directly into the interior, to visit a most interesting and typical *pueblo*, known as Ácoma. Arriving at the station nearest to it, early in the morning, we found a wagon and four horses waiting to receive us, and quickly started for our destination over a natural road across the almost level prairie. At the expiration of about two hours we saw before us, at a distance of three miles, a *mesa* of such perfect symmetry and brilliant pinkish color, that it called forth a unanimous expression of enthusiasm. Although the form of this "noblest single rock in America" changes as one beholds it from different points of view, the shape which it presented, as we approached it, was circular;

HOUSES AT LAGUNA.

and this, together with its uniform height and perpendicular walls, reminded me of the tomb of Cæcilia Metella on the Appian Way, magnified into majesty, as in a mirage. It was with added interest, therefore, that we learned that this was the Enchanted Mesa, about which there had been recently considerable scientific controversy. Enchanting, if not enchanted, it certainly appeared that morning, and, as we drew nearer, its imposing mass continued to suggest old Roman architecture, from Hadrian's Mausoleum by the Tiber to the huge circle of the Colosseum.

The Indian name of this remarkable cliff is *Katzímo*, and the title *Haunted Mesa* would be a more appropriate translation of the Spanish name, *Mesa Encantada*, than *Enchanted;* for the people of Ácoma believe its summit to be haunted by the spirits of their ancestors. A sinister tradition exists among them that one day, many centuries ago, when all the men of the village were at work upon the plain, a mass of rock, detached by the slow action of the elements, or else precipitated by an earthquake shock, fell into the narrow cleft by which alone an ascent or descent of the *mesa* was made,

THE MESA FROM THE EAST.

and rendered it impassable. The women and children, left thus on the summit of a cliff four hundred and thirty feet in height, and cut off from communication with their relatives and friends, who were unable to rejoin and rescue them, are said to have slowly perished by starvation, and their bones, pulverized in the course of centuries, are believed to have been, finally, blown or washed away. To test the truth of this tradition, at least so far as traces of a previous inhabitancy of the *mesa* could confirm it, Mr. Frederick W. Hodge, in 1895, made an attempt to reach the summit; but, though he climbed to within sixty feet of the top, he could on that occasion go no higher. He found, however, along the sides of the cliffs enormous masses of *débris*, washed down by the streams of water which, after a tempest, drain off from the summit in a thousand little cataracts. Not only did Mr. Hodge discover in

LOOKING THROUGH A CREVICE OF THE ENCHANTED MESA.

THE LYLE GUN AND ROPES.

this rubbish several fragments of Indian pottery, but he, also, observed certain holes in the cliff which seemed to him to have been cut there specially for hands and feet. These he believed to be traces of an ancient trail. Stimulated by the announcement of this discovery, Professor William Libbey, of Princeton College, in July, 1896, made the ascent of the Enchanted Mesa by means of a life line fired over the mound from a Lyle gun. Stout ropes having then been drawn over the cliffs and made secure, the adventurous aëronaut was actually hauled up to the summit in a boatswain's chair, as sailors are sometimes pulled ashore from a sinking ship. On his descent, however, he declared that he had found nothing to indicate that the crest had ever been inhabited, or even previously visited. Nothing

MAN IN BOATSWAIN'S CHAIR.

daunted by this statement, a few weeks later Mr. Hodge again attempted the ascent in which he had failed the year before. This time he was successful, and scaled the cliff by means of an extension ladder and several hundred feet of rope. But very different were the conclusions reached by

THE HODGE PARTY.

him as to the probable authenticity of the tradition; for after having been on the *mesa* only a short time, he found a piece of ancient pottery, and, during a search of twenty hours, not only were several more fragments of earthenware discovered, but also two stone ax-heads, an arrow-point of flint, and part of a shell bracelet. Moreover, a little monument of stone, arranged with evident design, was found on the edge of the cliff. Mr. Hodge and his party concluded, therefore, that beyond a doubt the Mesa Encantada had once been inhabited, and that the legend of the destruction of its last occupants may be true. The dis-

INDIAN RELICS.

covery of pieces of pottery here does not of itself prove great advancement in the race that made them; for, curiously enough, the manufacture of rude pottery is one of the first steps taken by man from a savage to a semi-civilized state. The various races of mankind have usually reached this art soon after their discovery of fire. In fact, such an invention is almost inevitable. Thus, an early method of cooking food has always been to put it into a basket smeared with clay, which is supported over a fire. The clay served the double purpose of preventing liquids from escaping and protecting the basket from the flame. Now, even the dullest savage could not have failed to notice, after a time, that the clay became hardened by the fire, and in that state was sufficient for his purpose without the basket. Simple as it seems, the discovery of this fact marks an important epoch in the progress of every primitive race, and some authorities on ethnology distinguish the two great divisions of Savagery and Barbarism by placing in the

THE TOP OF THE MESA ENCANTADA.

THE APPROACH TO ÁCOMA.

lower grade those who have not arrived at the knowledge of making pottery.

Soon after passing this haunted rock, and driving further over the *mesa*-dotted plain, we came in sight of the weird city of the sky called Ácoma. It occupies the summit of a table-land, the ascent to which is now a winding defile, flanked by frowning cliffs. Even this path, though readily ascended on horseback, is too precipitous and sandy for a wagon. Accordingly, as none of our party that day enjoyed the privilege of being an equestrian, we left our vehicle at the foot of the *mesa*, and completed the journey on foot. Some adventurous spirits, however, chose a short cut up the precipice along a natural fissure in the rocks, which, having been transformed with loose stones into a kind of ladder, was formerly, before these peaceful times, the only means of access to the summit. A steeper scramble would be hard to find. I must confess, however, that before taking either of these routes, we halted to enjoy a lunch for which the drive had given us the keenest appetite, and which we ate *al fresco* in the shadow of a cliff, surrounded by a dozen curious natives. Then, the imperious demands of hunger satisfied, we climbed three hundred and fifty feet above the surrounding plain, and stood in what is, with perhaps the exception of Zuñi, the oldest inhabited town in North America. Before us, on what seemed to be an island of the air, was a perfect specimen of the aboriginal civilization found here by the Spanish conqueror, Coronado, and his eager gold-seekers, in 1540. For now, as then, the members of the tribe reside together in one immense community building. It is rather droll to find among these natives of the desert the idea of the modern apartment house; but, in this place, as in all the settlements of the Pueblo Indians, communal dwellings were in existence long before the discovery of America, and the *mesa* of Ácoma was inhabited as it now is, when the Pilgrims landed upon Plymouth Rock.

RAIN WATER BASIN, ÁCOMA.

An Indian *pueblo* is really a honeycomb of adobe cells, built up in terraces. The outer walls, being the most exposed, are the highest, and from them toward the centre of the village, projecting stories descend in such a way that the balcony of one series of rooms forms a roof for the next below it. Finally, in the heart of the *pueblo* is an open area where horses are coralled. When the space on the summit of the *mesa* is sufficient, these apartment dwellings may be increased indefinitely by adding cells to the original mass, till it is six or seven stories high, and may contain one hundred, five hundred, or even a thousand persons, according to the size of the tribe. Formerly there were no doorways in the lowest stories; but in these peaceful days they are now introduced occasionally by Indian architects. Where they do not exist, the only means of entering the ground-floor rooms is by climbing a ladder from the courtyard to the first terrace, and thence descending by another ladder through a hole in the roof. The upper stories, being safer from attack, are more liberally supplied with doors

THE COURTYARD OF ÁCOMA.

HOUSE OF A PUEBLO CHIEF.

and windows, the latter being sometimes glazed with plates of mica. At present, panes of glass are also used, though they were pointed out to us as special luxuries. At night, and in times of danger, the ladders in these *pueblos* used always to be drawn up after the last climbers had used them; since these industrious and sedentary Indians were ever liable to raids from their nomadic enemies, who coveted their stores of food and the few treasures they had gradually accumulated. This precaution on the part of the Pueblos again reminds us that human nature, in its primitive devices for self-protection, is everywhere very

A GROUP OF PUEBLO INDIANS.

A PUEBLO TOWN.

much the same. Thus, there is no connection between the Swiss Lake Dwellers and the Indians of New Mexico; yet as the latter, on retiring to their houses, draw up their ladders after them, so the old occupants of the villages built on piles in the Swiss lakes pulled after them at night the bridges which connected them with the land.

One can well imagine that the people of Ácoma do not spend many of their waking hours in their apartments. In this warm climate, with its superb air and almost rainless sky, every one lives as much as possible out of doors, and a true child of the sun always prefers the canopy of heaven to any other covering, and would rather eat on his doorstep and sleep on his flat roof, than to dine at a sumptuous table or recline on a comfortable bed. Nature seems to be peculiarly kind and indulgent to the people of warm climates. They need not only less clothing but less food, and it is only when we travel in the tropics that we realize on how little sustenance man can exist. A few dates, a cup of coffee, and a bit of bread appear to satisfy the appetites of most Aridians, whether they are Indians

CHARACTERISTIC PUEBLO HOUSES.

or Arabs. In the North, food, clothing, and fire are necessities of life; but to the people of the South the sun suffices for a furnace, fruits give sufficient nourishment, and clothing is a chance acquaintance. Yet life is full of compensation. Where Nature is too indulgent, her favorites grow shiftless; and the greatest amount of indoor luxury and comfort is always found where Nature seems so hostile that man is forced to fight with her for life.

Most of the cells which we examined in the many-chambered

IN THE PUEBLO.

honeycomb of Ácoma had very little furniture except a primitive table and a few stools, made out of blocks of wood or trunks of trees. Across one corner of each room was, usually, stretched a cord on which the articles of the family wardrobe had been thrown promiscuously. The ornaments visible were usually bows and arrows, rifles, Navajo blankets, and leather pouches, hung on wooden pegs. Of beds I could find none; for Indians sleep by preference on blankets, skins, or coarse-wool mattresses spread every night upon the floor. When we consider that the forty millions of Japan, even in their comparatively high degree of civilization, still sleep in much the same way, we realize how unnecessary bedsteads are to the majority of the human race. In a few rooms I discovered wooden statuettes of saints, one or two crucifixes, and some cheap prints, which were evidently regarded with great veneration. The floors, which were not of wood, but of smooth adobe nearly as hard as asphalt, were in every instance remarkably clean.

It is an interesting fact, in the domestic economy of the Indian life led in these aërial villages, that the woman is always the complete owner of her apartment and its contents; for it is the women of the tribe who build the dwellings. Accordingly, the position of a Pueblo woman is extraordinary; and should her husband ill-treat her, she has the right and power to evict him, and to send him back to his original home. On the other hand, the man is sole possessor of the live stock of the family and of the property in the field; but when the crops are housed, the wife is at once invested with an equal share in their ownership. Pueblo children, too, always trace their descent through the mother and take her clan name instead of the father's. I noticed that at Ácoma the children

INTERIOR OF A PUEBLO APARTMENT.

seemed to be obedient to their parents and respectful to age, as I have invariably found them to be in all partially civilized countries of the world; for, paradoxical as it may seem, it is only in highly civilized communities, where individualism is cultivated at the expense of strict discipline and parental control, that children become indifferent to their fathers and mothers, and insolent to their superiors in age and wisdom.

PUEBLO WATER-CARRIERS.

We lingered for some time upon this citadel of Ácoma, profoundly interested in the life and customs of a people that asks no aid of the United States, but is, to-day, as self-supporting as it has always been. The number of Pueblo Indians was never very large. It is probable that there were in all about thirty thousand of them at the time of the Spanish conquest, in 1540, and there are now about one-third that number scattered through more than twenty settlements. In an arid land where the greatest need is water, it is not strange that the dwellers on these rocky eyries should be called in the Indian dialect "Drinkers of the dew," for it would seem as if the dew must be their only beverage. But there are springs upon the neighboring plains whose precious liquid is brought up the steep trail daily on the heads of women, in three or five gallon jars, the carrying of which gives to the poise of the head and neck a native grace and elegance, as characteristic of Pueblo women as of the girls of Capri. Moreover, on the summit of the *mesa* there are, usually, hollows in the rock, partly natural, partly artificial, which serve as reservoirs to retain rain water and keep it fresh and cool.

AN ESTUFA.

Besides the communal apartment-house, every *pueblo* contains two characteristic edifices. One is as ancient as the tribe itself and thoroughly aboriginal, the other is comparatively modern and bears the imprint of the Spaniard; they are the *estufa* and the Roman Catholic church. The *estufa* has always played a prominent part in the history of these Indians. It is a semi-subterranean council hall, where matters of public business are discussed by the chiefs. The government of the Pueblos is practically the same as when the Spanish found them. Each village seems to be completely independent of its neighbors, and no member of one tribe is allowed to sell real estate to members of another, or to marry into another clan without permission from his own. Each settlement is governed by a council, the members of which, including its chief, are chosen annually. Heredity counts

ESTUFA AND SURROUNDINGS.

for nothing among them, and official positions are conferred only by popular vote. Even their war-chieftains are elected and are under the control of the council. All matters of public importance are discussed by this body in the *estufa*, the walls of which are usually whitewashed; but a more dismal place can hardly be imagined, not only from the dubious light which there prevails, but from the fact that it contains no furniture whatever, and no decoration. Sometimes a village will have several *estufas*, each being reserved for a separate clan of the tribe. In any case, whether many or few, they are used exclusively by men, women never being allowed to enter them except to bring food to their male relatives. As we approached the Ácoma *estufa*, it presented the appearance of a monstrous bean pot, from the opening of which a ladder rose to a height of twenty feet. This proved to be the only means of descending into an enclosure, to which we were politely but firmly denied admission. Peering

MEXICAN OVENS.

into the aperture, however, and noting the warm, close air which came from it, I understood why the Spanish word *estufa*, or oven, was applied to these underground cells by their European discoverers; for neither light nor ventilation is obtainable except through the one opening, and in summer the temperature of the shallow cavern must be warm indeed.

The only other notable structure in Ácoma is the Roman Catholic church, the walls of which are sixty feet in height and ten feet thick. One can realize the enormous amount of labor involved in its construction, when he reflects that every stone and every piece of timber used in building it had to be brought hither on the backs of Indians, over the plains, from a considerable distance, and up the desperately difficult and narrow trail. Even the graveyard, which occupies a space in front of the church, about two hundred feet square, is said to have required a labor of forty years, since the cemetery had to be enclosed with stone walls, forty feet deep at one edge and filled with earth brought in small basket-loads up the steep ascent from the plain below. The

THE OLD CHURCH AT ÁCOMA.

THE ALTAR.

church itself is regarded by the Indians with the utmost reverence, although it must be said that their religion is still almost as much Pagan as Christian. Thus, while they respect the priests who come to minister to them, they also have a lurking reverence for the medicine man, who is known as the *cacique*. He is really the religious head of the community, a kind of augur and prophet, who consults the gods and communicates to the people the answers he claims to have received. This dignitary is exempt from all work of a manual kind, such as farming, digging irrigation-ditches, and even hunting, and receives compensation for his services in the form of a tract of land which the community cultivates for him with more care than is bestowed on any other portion of their territory, while his crops are the first harvested in the autumn. He also derives an income in the form of grain, buckskin, shells, or turquoises, from those who beg him to fast for them, and to intercede with the gods in case of sickness. On the other hand, the *cacique* must lodge and feed all the strangers who come to the village, as long as they stay, and he is, also, the surgeon and the nurse of the community.

While, therefore, the Pueblos go to church and repeat prayers in accordance with Christian teaching, they also use the prayer-sticks of their ancestors, and still place great reliance on their dances, most of which are of a strictly religious character, and are not only dedicated to the sun, moon, rainbow, deer, elk, and sheep, but are usually performed for the specific purpose of obtaining rain. Formerly, too, when their lives were far less peaceful than they are to-day, the Pueblos indulged in war and scalp dances; but these are now falling into disuse. The most remarkable exhibition of dancing, still in vogue, is the repulsive Snake Dance of the Moquis of Arizona, which takes place every year alternately in four villages between the 10th and the 30th of August according to the phase of the moon. The origin of this extraordinary custom is not intelligible now even to the Indians themselves, but the object in performing it is to obtain rain, and the dance, itself, is the culmination of a religious ceremonial which continues for nine days and nights. During that time only those who have been initi-

DANCE IN THE PUEBLO.

PUEBLO GIRLS.

THREE SNAKE PRIESTS.

ated into the Sacred Fraternities of the tribe may enter the *estufa*, on the floor of which weird pictures have been made with colored sand.

In the tribe of Moquis there are two fraternities known as the Antelopes and the Snakes. Each has from twenty to thirty members, some of whom are boys who serve as acolytes. When the open air ceremony of the Snake Dance begins, the members of these brotherhoods appear scantily clothed, with their faces painted red and white, and with tortoise-shell rattles tied to their legs. The Antelope fraternity first enters the square, preceded by a venerable priest carrying two bags filled with snakes. These serpents, which have been previously washed and covered with sacred meal, are deposited by the priest in a small leaf-embowered enclosure called the *kisi*. Around this the Antelopes now march, stamping with the right foot violently, to notify the spirits of their ancestors (presumably in the lower world) that the ceremony has begun. After making the circuit of the enclosure four times, they halt, and stand in line with their backs turned toward it. Then the Snake fraternity ap-

THE SNAKE DANCE.

pears, headed by its priest, and performs the same ceremony. Then they too form a line, facing the Antelopes, and all of them, for about five minutes, wave their wands and chant some unintelligible words. Suddenly one Antelope and one Snake man rush to the *kisi*, and the priest who is presiding over the serpents presents them with a snake. The Snake man immediately places the wriggling reptile in his mouth, and holds it by the centre of its body between his teeth, as he marches around the little plaza, taking high steps. Meantime the Antelope man accompanies him, stroking the snake continually with a wand tipped with feathers. Then all the members of the two fraternities follow in couples and do the same thing. Finally, each Snake man carries at least two snakes in his mouth and several in his hands; and even little boys, five years old, dressed like the adults, also hold snakes in their hands, fearlessly. Once in a while a snake is purposely dropped, and a man whose special duty it is to prevent its escape rushes after it and catches it up.

All the time that this hideous ceremony is going on, a weird chant is sung by the men and women of the tribe; and, at last, the chief priest draws on the ground a mystic circle with a line of sacred meal, and into this the men unload their snakes until the whole space becomes a writhing mass of serpents. Suddenly the members rush into this throng of squirming reptiles, most of which are rattlesnakes, and each, grabbing up a handful of them, runs at full speed down the *mesa* and sets them at liberty, to act as messengers to carry to the gods their prayers for rain. This ends the ceremony for the snakes, but not for the men; for after they have liberated the reptiles, the members of the brotherhoods return and bathe themselves in a kind of green decoction, called Frog-water. Then they drink a powerful emetic, and having lined up on the edge of the *mesa*, vomit in unison! This is to purge them from the evil effects of snake-handling; and lest it should not be sufficiently effectual, the dose is repeated. Then they sit down, and eat bread, given them by the women as a kind of communion or religious rite.

AFTER THE EMETIC.

CHIEF SNAKE PRIEST.

The seventy or eighty snakes used in this dance are treated from first to last with the utmost kindness and respect, especially the rattlesnakes, a dozen of which will frequently be squirming on the ground at once. It is noticeable that the Indians never pick up a rattlesnake when coiled, but always wait until it straightens itself out under the feather stroking, for it is claimed that the rattlesnake cannot strike uncoiled. At all events, when one is at its full length, the Indians not only catch it up fearlessly, but carry it with impunity in their mouths and hands. As might be supposed, however, the Moquis are said to possess an antidote against the poison of a rattlesnake, which, if a man is bitten, is given to him at once; and it is said that none of them ever dies from the effects of a snake-bite.

WHERE THE SNAKES ARE KEPT.

The religious element in all these ceremonies should not be lost sight of, for the life of the Pueblo In-

RELICS OF CLIFF DWELLERS.

dians is permeated with religion, or superstition, to the minutest details. Thus, it is an interesting fact that vicarious atonement has been a custom among them from time immemorial, and their *cacique* is compelled to fast and do penance in many ways for the sins of his people. In some of the villages, also, certain men and women are chosen to expiate the wrongdoings of the tribe; and for more than a century there has been in New Mexico an order of Penitents, who torture themselves by beating their bodies with

SUMMIT OF A MOQUI MESA.

sharp cactus thorns, by carrying heavy crosses for great distances, and even by actual crucifixion. The severest of these cruel rites have, finally, been suppressed by the Roman Catholic church, but it encountered great difficulty in so doing, and the last crucifixion took place in 1891.

Such, then, are the Pueblos of New Mexico and Arizona; a race uniting aboriginal Pagan rites with Christian ceremonies: cherishing at the same time their idols and their churches; using to-day their rifles, and to-morrow their bows and arrows; pounding occasionally with a hammer, but preferably with a stone; and handling American money for certain purchases, while trading beads, shells, and turquoises for others. Sometimes we wonder that they have not made more progress during the cen-

MOQUI CART AND PLOW.

turies in which they have been associated with Europeans; but it is hard to realize the difficulties which they have encountered in trying to comprehend our civilization, and in grasping its improvements. Even the adoption of the antique Spanish plow, the clumsy two-wheeled cart, the heavy ax and the rude saw, which are still found among them, caused them to pass at one stride from the Stone to the Iron Age, which, but for the intervention of the Spaniards, they would not naturally have reached without centuries of patient plodding. Moreover, before the arrival of the Europeans, the Aborigines of America had never seen horses, cows, sheep, or dogs, and the turkey was the only domestic animal known to them. Hence, in ancient American society there was no such thing as a pastoral stage of development; and the absence of domestic animals from the western hemisphere is a very important reason why the progress of mankind in this part of the world was not more rapid. Still it is a remarkable fact that the most ancient race, of which we have any actual knowledge on this continent, is, also, the most peaceful, self-supporting, and industrious, subsisting principally on the sale of their curiously decorated pottery, and the products of their arid soil. We saw here a young man who had been educated in the Government School at Carlisle; but, like most of his race, after returning to his village he had reverted to the ways of his ancestors, disqualified by his birth and instincts of heredity from doing anything else successfully.

It was late on the night succeeding our visit to Ácoma that we arrived at Flagstaff, and our entire party was asleep. Suddenly we were aroused by a prolonged shout and the discharge of half a dozen revolvers. Five minutes later there came a general fusillade of pistol shots, and near and distant cries were heard, in which our half-awakened faculties could distinguish only the words: "Hurry up!" "Call the crowd!" "Down

MOQUI CHILDREN.

FLAGSTAFF STATION.

the alley!" Then a gruff voice yelled just beneath my window: "Let her go," and instantly our locomotive gave a whistle so piercing and continuous that all the occupants of our car sprang from their couches, and met in a demoralized group of multi-colored pajamas in the corridor. What was it? Had the train been held up? Were we attacked? No; both the whistle and the pistol shots were merely Flagstaff's mode of giving an alarm of fire. We hastily dressed and stepped out upon the platform. A block of buildings just opposite the station was on fire, and was evidently doomed; yet Flagstaff's citizens, whose forms, relieved against the lurid glow, looked like Comanche Indians in a war dance, fought the flames with stubborn fury. The sight of a successful conflagration always thrills me, partly with horror, partly with delight. Three hundred feet away, two buildings formed an ever-increasing pyramid of golden light. We could distinguish the thin streams of water thrown by two

PACKING WOOD.

puny engines; but, in comparison with the great tongues of fire which they strove to conquer, they appeared like silver straws. Nothing could check the mad carousal of the sparks and flames, which danced, leaped, whirled, reversed, and intertwined, like demons waltzing with a company of witches on Walpurgis Night. A few adventurous men climbed to the roofs of the adjoining structures, and thence poured buckets of water on the angry holocaust; but, for all the good they thus accomplished, they might as well have spat upon the surging, writhing fire, which flashed up in their faces like exploding bombs, whenever por-

A MEXICAN HOME.

tions of the buildings fell. Meantime huge clouds of dense smoke, scintillant with sparks, rolled heavenward from this miniature Vesuvius; the neighboring windows, as they caught the light, sparkled like monster jewels; two telegraph poles caught fire, and cut their slender forms and outstretched arms against the jet black sky, like gibbets made of gold. How fire and water serve us, when subdued as slaves; but, oh, how terribly they scourge us, if ever for a moment they can gain the mastery! Too interested to exchange a word, we watched the struggle and awaited the result. The fury of the fire seemed like the wild attack of Indians, inflamed with frenzy and fanaticism, sure to exhaust itself at last, but for the moment riotously triumphant. Gradually, however, through want of material on which to feed itself, the fiery demon drooped its shining crest, brandished its arms with lessening vigor, and seemed to writhe convulsively, as thrust after thrust from the silver spears of its assailants reached a vital spot. Finally, after hurling one last shower of firebrands, it sank back into darkness, and its hereditary enemy rushed in to drown each lingering spark of its reduced vitality.

OUR CAR AT FLAGSTAFF.

THE HEAVENS FROM THE OBSERVATORY, FLAGSTAFF.

Upon a hill near Flagstaff stands an astronomical observatory from which distinguished students of the midnight skies search for the secrets of the moon and stars. Few better sites on earth could have been chosen for this purpose, since Arizona's atmosphere is so transparent that the extent of celestial scenery here disclosed is extraordinary. We visited the structure at the solemn hour that marks the hush between two days, when the last sound of one has died away, and before the first stir of the other thrills the morning air. Then, gazing through the lenses of its noble telescope, we welcomed the swift waves of light pulsating toward us from the shoreless ocean we call space. There is a mysterious beauty about the radiance of a star that far surpasses that of the moon. The latter glitters only with reflected light; but a star (that is to say a distant sun), when seen through a telescope, frequently scintillates with different colors like a diamond, and quivers like a thing of life. Moreover, the moon, forever waxing, waning, or presenting almost stupidly its great flat face, is continually changing; but the fixed star is always there. It fills the thoughtful

TWILIGHT.

soul with awe to look upon the starry heavens through such an instrument as that at Flagstaff. Space for the moment seems annihilated. We are apparently transported, as observers, from our tiny planet to the confines of our solar system, and, gazing thence still farther toward infinity, we watch with bated breath the birth, the progress, and the death of worlds. To one of the most distant objects in the depths of space, known as the Ring Nebula, the author addressed the following lines:

TO THE RING NEBULA.

O, pallid spectre of the midnight skies!
  Whose phantom features in the dome of Night
Elude the keenest gaze of wistful eyes
  Till amplest lenses aid the failing sight,
On heaven's blue sea the farthest isle of fire,
From thee, whose glories it would fain admire,
Must vision, baffled, in despair retire!

What art thou, ghostly visitant of flame?
  Wouldst thou 'neath closer scrutiny dissolve
In myriad suns that constellations frame,
  Round which life-freighted satellites revolve,
Like those unnumbered orbs which nightly creep
In dim procession o'er the azure steep,
As white-wing'd caravans the desert sweep?

THE SAN FRANCISCO VOLCANOES.

Or, art thou still an incandescent mass,
  Acquiring form as hostile forces urge,
Through whose vast length a million lightnings pass
  As to and fro its fiery billows surge,
Whose glowing atoms, whirled in ceaseless strife
Where now chaotic anarchy is rife,
Shall yet become the fair abodes of life?

We know not; for the faint, exhausted rays
  Which hither on Light's wingèd coursers come
From fires which ages since first lit their blaze,
  One instant gleam, then perish, spent and dumb!
How strange the thought that, whatsoe'er we learn,
Our tiny globe no answer can return,
Since with but dull, reflected beams we burn!

Yet this we know; yon ring of spectral light,
  Whose distance thrills the soul with solemn awe,
Can ne'er escape in its majestic might
  The firm control of omnipresent law.
This mote descending to its bounden place,
Those suns whose radiance we can scarcely trace,
Alike obey the Power pervading space.

NIGHT.

One glorious September morning, leaving our train at Flagstaff, we started in stage-coaches for a drive of sixty-five miles to the Grand Cañon. I had looked forward to this drive with some misgiving, dreading the heat of the sun, and the dust and sand which I had supposed we should encounter; but to my astonishment and delight it was a thoroughly enjoyable experience. It was only eleven hours in duration, and not only was most of the route level, but two-thirds of it lay through a section of beautifully rolling land, diversified with open glades and thousands upon thousands of tall pines and cedars entirely free from undergrowth. It is no exaggeration to say that we drove that day for miles at a time over a road carpeted with pine needles. The truth is, Arizona, though usually considered a treeless and rainless country, possesses some remarkable exceptions; and the region near Flagstaff not only abounds in stately pines, but is at certain seasons visited by rainstorms which keep it fresh and beautiful. During our stay at the

STARTING FOR THE GRAND CAÑON.

THE DRIVE THROUGH THE PINES.

Grand Cañon we had a shower every night; the atmosphere was marvelously pure, and aromatic with the odors of a million pines; and so exhilarating was exercise in the open air, that however arduous it might be, we never felt inconvenienced by fatigue, and mere existence gave us joy. Decidedly, then, it will not do to condemn the whole of Arizona because of the heat of its arid, southern plains; for the northern portion of the state is a plateau, with an elevation of from five thousand to seven thousand feet. Hence, as it is not latitude, so much as altitude, that gives us healthful, pleasing temperature, in parts of Arizona the climate is delightful during the entire year.

A portion of this stage-coach journey led us over the flank of the great San Francisco Mountain. The isolated position, striking similarity, and almost uniform altitude of its four peaks, rising nearly thirteen thousand feet above the sea, have long

THE SAN FRANCISCO MOUNTAIN.

made them famous. Moreover, they are memorable for having cast a lurid light upon the development of this portion of our planet. Cold, calm, and harmless though they now appear, the time has been when they contained a molten mass which needed but a throb of Earth's uneasy heart to light the heavens with an angry glare, and cover the adjoining plains with floods of fire. Lava has often poured from their destructive cones, and can be traced thence over a distance of thirty miles; proving that they once served as vents for the volcanic force which the thin crust of earth was vainly striving to confine. But their activity is apparently ended. The voices with which they formerly shouted to one another in the joy of devastation have been silenced. Conquered at last, their fires smolder now beneath a barrier too firm to yield, and their huge forms appear like funeral monuments reared to the memory of the power buried at their base. Another fascinating sight upon this drive was that of the

Painted Desert whose variously colored streaks of sand, succeeding one another to the rim of the horizon, made the vast area seem paved with bands of onyx, agate, and carnelian.

About the hour of noon we reached a lunch-station at which the stages, going to and from the Cañon, meet and pass. The structure itself is rather primitive; but a good meal is served to tourists at this wayside halting-place, and since our appetites had been sharpened by the long ride and tonic-giving air, it seemed to us the most delicious of repasts. The principal object of one of the members of our party, in making the journey described in these pages, was to determine the advisability of building a railroad from Flagstaff to the Cañon. Whether this will be done eventually is not, however, a matter of vital interest to travelers, since the country traversed can easily be made an almost ideal coaching-route; and with good stages, frequent relays of horses, and a well-appointed lunch-station, a journey thus accomplished would be preferable to a trip by rail.*

* This railroad has now become an accomplished fact, and runs from the main line at Williams directly to the Cañon, near the brink of which a fine hotel has been constructed.

THE LUNCH-STATION.

Night had already come when we arrived at our destination, known as Hance's Camp, near the border of the Cañon. As we drove up to it, the situation seemed enchanting in its peace and beauty; for it is located in a grove of noble pines, through which the moon that night looked down in full-orbed splendor, paving the turf with inlaid ebony and silver, and laying a mantle of white velvet on the tents in which we were to sleep. Hance's log cabin serves as a kitchen and dining-room for trav-

HANCE'S CAMP.

elers, and a few guests can even find lodging there; but, until a hotel is built, the principal dormitories must be the tents, which are provided with wooden floors and furnished with tables, chairs, and comfortable beds. This kind of accommodation, however, although excellent for travelers in robust health, is not sufficiently luxurious to attract many tourists. The evident necessity of the place is a commodious, well-kept inn, situated a few hundred feet to the rear of Hance's Camp,

OUR TENT AT HANCE'S CAMP.

on the very edge of the Cañon. If such a hotel, built on a spot commanding the incomparable view, were properly advertised and well-managed, I firmly believe that thousands of people would come here every year, on their way to or from the Pacific coast—not wishing or expecting it to be a place of fashion, but seeking it as a point where, close beside a park of pines, seven thousand feet above the level of the sea, one of the greatest marvels of the world can be enjoyed, in all the different phases it presents at morning, noon, and night, in sunshine, moonlight, and in storm.

OLD HANCE.

Early the next morning I eagerly climbed the little knoll at the foot of which our tents were located, for I well knew that from its summit I should see the Cañon. Many grand objects in the world are heralded by sound: the solemn music of Niagara, the roar of active geysers in the Yellowstone, the intermittent thunder of the sea upon a rocky coast, are all distinguishable at some distance; but over the Grand Cañon of the Colorado broods a solemn silence. No warning voice proclaims its close proximity; no partial view prepares us for its awful presence. We walk a few steps through the pine trees from the camp and suddenly find ourselves upon the Cañon's edge. Just before reaching it, I halted for a moment, as has always been my wont when approaching for the first time any natural or historic object that I have longed for years to look upon. Around me rose the stately pines; behind me was a simple stretch of rolling woodland; nothing betrayed the nearness of one of the greatest wonders of the world. Could it

THE FIRST VIEW.

THE EARTH-GULF OF ARIZONA.

A PORTION OF THE GULF.

be possible that I was to be disappointed? At last I hurried through the intervening space, gave a quick look, and almost reeled. The globe itself seemed to have suddenly yawned asunder, leaving me trembling on the hither brink of two dissevered hemispheres. Vast as the bed of a vanished ocean, deep as Mount Washington, riven from its apex to its base, the grandest cañon on our planet lay glittering below me in the sunlight like a submerged continent, drowned by an ocean that had ebbed away. At my very feet, so near that I could have leaped at once into eternity, the earth was cleft to a depth of six thousand six hundred feet — not by a narrow gorge, like other cañons, but by an awful gulf within whose cavernous immensity the forests of the Adirondacks would appear like jackstraws, the Hudson Palisades would be an insignificant stratum, Niagara would be indiscernible, and cities could be tossed like pebbles.

"A VAST, INCOMPARABLE VOID."

As brain grew steadier and vision clearer, I saw, directly opposite, the other side of the Cañon thirteen miles away. It was a mountain wall, a mile in height, extending to the right and left as far as the eye could reach; and since the cliff upon which I was standing was its counterpart, it seemed to me as if these parallel banks were once the shore-lines of a vanished sea. Between them lay a vast, incomparable void, two hundred miles in length, presenting an unbroken panorama to the east and west until the gaze could follow it no farther. Try to conceive what these dimensions mean by realizing that a strip of the State of Massachusetts, thirteen miles in width, and reaching from Boston to Albany, could be laid as a covering over this Cañon, from one end to the other; and that if the entire range of the White Mountains were flung into it, the monstrous pit would still remain comparatively empty! Even now it is by no means without contents; for, as I gazed with awe and wonder into its colossal area, I seemed to be looking down upon a colored relief-map of the mountain systems of the continent. It is not strictly one cañon, but a labyrinth of cañons, in many of which the whole Yosemite could be packed away and lost. Thus one of them, the Marble Cañon, is of itself more than three thousand feet deep and sixty-six miles long. In every direction I beheld below me a tangled skein of mountain ranges, thousands of feet in height, which the Grand Cañon's walls enclosed, as if it were a huge sarcophagus, holding the skeleton of an infant world. It is evident, therefore, that all the other cañons of our globe are, in comparison with this, what pygmies are to a giant, and that the name Grand Cañon, which is often used to designate some relatively

A SECTION OF THE LABYRINTH.

MOUNT AYER.

insignificant ravine, should be in truth applied only to the stupendous earth-gulf of Arizona.

At length, I began to try to separate and identify some of these formations. Directly in the foreground, a savage looking mountain reared its splintered head from the abyss, and stood defiantly confronting me, six thousand feet above the Cañon's floor. Though practically inaccessible to the average tourist, this has been climbed, and is named Mount Ayer, after Mrs. Edward Ayer, the first woman who ever descended into the Cañon to the river's edge. Beyond this, other mountains rise from the gulf, many of which resemble the Step Pyramid at Sakhara, one of the oldest of the royal sepulchres beside the Nile. But so immeasurably vaster are the pyramids of this Cañon than any work of man, that had the tombs of the Pharaohs been placed beside them, I could not have discovered them without a field-glass. Some of these grand constructions stand alone, while others are in pairs; and many of them resemble Oriental temples, buttressed with terraces a mile or two in length, and approached by steps a hundred feet in height. Around these, too, are many smaller mountainous formations, crude and unfinished in appearance, like shrines commenced and then abandoned by the Cañon's Architect. Most of us are but children of a larger growth, and love to interpret Nature, as if she reared her mountains, painted her sunsets, cut her cañons, and poured forth her cataracts solely for our instruction and enjoyment. So, when we gaze on forms like these, shaped like gigantic temples, obelisks, and altars fashioned by man's hands, we try to see behind them something personal, and even name them after Hindu, Grecian, and Egyptian gods, as if those deities made them their abodes. Thus, one of these shrines was called by the artist, Thomas Moran, the Temple of Set; three others are dedicated respectively to

SOME OF THE CAÑON TEMPLES.

SIVA'S TEMPLE.

Siva, Vishnu, and Vulcan; while on the apex of a mighty altar, still unnamed, a twisted rock-formation, several hundred feet in height, suggests a flame, eternally preserved by unseen hands, ascending to an unknown god.

It is difficult to realize the magnitude of these objects, so deceptive are distances and dimensions in the transparent atmosphere of Arizona. Siva's Temple, for example, stands upon a platform four or five miles square, from which rise domes and pinnacles a thousand feet in height. Some of their summits call to mind immense sarcophagi of jasper or of porphyry, as if they were the burial-places of dead deities, and the Grand Cañon a Necropolis for pagan gods. Yet, though the greater part of the population of the world could be assembled here, one sees no worshipers, save an occasional devotee of Nature, standing on the Cañon's rim, lost in astonishment and hushed in awe. These temples were, however, never intended for a human priesthood. A man beside them is a pygmy. His voice here would be little more effective than the chirping of an insect. The God-appointed celebrant, in the cathedrals of this Cañon, must be Nature. Her voice alone can rouse the echoes of these mountains into deafening peals of thunder. Her metaphors are drawn from an experience of ages. Her prayers are silent, rapturous communings with the Infinite. Her hymns of praise are the glad songs of birds; her requiems are the moanings of the pines; her symphonies the solemn roaring of the winds. "Sermons in stone" abound at every turn; and if, as the poet has affirmed, "An undevout astronomer is mad," with still more truth can it be said that those are blind who in this wonderful environment look not "through Nature up to Nature's God." These wrecks of Tempest and of Time are finger-posts that point the thoughts of mortals to eternal heights; and we find cause for hope in the fact that, even in a place like this, Man is superior to Nature; for he interprets it, he finds in it the thoughts of God, and reads them after Him.

NEAR THE TEMPLE OF SET.

HANCE'S TRAIL, LOOKING UP.

The coloring of the Grand Cañon is no less extraordinary than its forms. Nature has saved this chasm from being a terrific scene of desolation by glorifying all that it contains. Wall after wall, turret after turret, and mountain range after mountain range, belted with tinted strata, succeed one another here like billows petrified in glowing colors. These hues are not as brilliant and astonishing in their variety as are the colors of the Yellowstone Cañon, but their subdued and sombre tones are perfectly suited to the awe-inspiring place which they adorn. The prominent tints are yellow, red, maroon, and a dull purple, as if the glory of unnumbered sunsets, fading from these rugged cliffs, had been in part imprisoned here. Yet, somehow, specimens of these colored rocks lose all their brilliancy and beauty when removed from their environment, like sea-shells from the beach; a verification of the sentiment so beautifully expressed in the lines of Emerson:

"I wiped away the weeds and foam,
I fetched my sea-born treasures home;
But the poor, unsightly, noisome things
Had left their beauty on the shore,
With the sun and the sand and the wild uproar."

To stand upon the edge of this stupendous gorge, as it receives its earliest greeting from the god of day, is to enjoy in a moment compensation for long years of ordinary uneventful life. When I beheld the scene, a little before daybreak, a lake of soft, white clouds was floating round the summits of the Cañon mountains, hiding the huge crevasse beneath, as a light coverlet of snow conceals a chasm in an Alpine glacier. I looked with awe upon this misty curtain of the morn, for it appeared to me symbolic of the grander curtain of the past which shuts out from our view the awful struggles of the elements enacted here when the grand gulf was being formed. At length, however, as the light increased, this thin, diaphanous

MIST IN THE CAÑON.

covering was mysteriously withdrawn, and when the sun's disk rose above the horizon, the huge façades of the temples which looked eastward grew immediately rosy with the dawn; westward, projecting cliffs sketched on the opposite sides of the ravines, in dark blue silhouettes, the evanescent forms of castles, battlements, and turrets from which some shreds of white mist waved like banners of capitulation; stupendous moats beneath them were still black with shadow; while clouds filled many of the minor cañons, like vapors rising from enormous caldrons. Gradually, as the solar couriers forced a passage into the narrow gullies, and drove the remnant of night's army from its hiding-places, innumerable shades of purple, yellow, red, and brown appeared, varying according to the composition of the mountains, and the enormous void was gradually filled to the brim with a luminous haze, which one could fancy was the smoke of incense from its countless altars. A similar, and even more impressive, scene is visible here in the late afternoon,

A STUPENDOUS PANORAMA.

A TANGLED SKEIN OF CAÑONS.

when all the western battlements in their turn grow resplendent, while the eastern walls submit to an eclipse; till, finally, a gray pall drops upon the lingering bloom of day, the pageant fades, the huge sarcophagi are mantled in their shrouds, the gorgeous colors which have blazed so sumptuously through the day grow pale and vanish, the altar fires turn to ashes, the mighty temples draw their veils and seem deserted by both gods and men, and the stupendous panorama awaits, beneath the canopy of night, the glory of another dawn.

It was my memorable privilege to see, one afternoon, a thunder storm below me here. A monstrous cloud-wall, like a huge gray veil, came traveling up the Cañon, and we could watch the lightning strike the buttes and domes ten or twelve miles away, while the loud peals of thunder, broken by crags and multiplied by echoes, rolled toward us through the darkening gulf at steadily decreasing intervals. Sometimes two flashes at a time ran quivering through the air and launched their bolts upon the mountain shrines, as though their altars, having been erected for idolatrous worship, were doomed to be annihilated. Occasionally, through an opening in the clouds, the sun would suddenly light up the summit of a mountain, or flash a path of gold through a ravine; and I shall never forget the curious sensation of seeing far beneath me bright sunshine in one cañon and a violent storm in another. At last, a rainbow cast its radiant bridge across the entire space, and we beheld the tempest disappear like a troop of cavalry in a cloud of dust beneath that iridescent arch, beyond whose curving spectrum all the temples stood forth, still intact in their sublimity.

At certain points along the Cañon, promontories jut out into the abyss, like headlands which in former times projected into an ocean that has disappeared.
Hence, riding along the brink,

ON THE BRINK.

RIPLEY'S BUTTE.

as one may do for miles, we looked repeatedly into many lateral fissures, from fifteen hundred to three thousand feet in depth. All these, however, like gigantic fingers, pointed downward to the centre of the Cañon, where, five miles away, and at a level more than six thousand feet below the brink on which we stood, extended a long, glittering trail. This, where the sunlight struck it, gleamed like an outstretched band of gold. It was the sinuous Colorado, yellow as the Tiber.

A BIT OF THE RIVER.

One day of our stay here was devoted to making the descent to this river. It is an undertaking compared with which the crossing of the Gemmi on a mule is child's play. Fortunately, however, the arduous trip is not absolutely necessary for an appreciation of the immensity and grandeur of the scenery. On the contrary, one gains a really better idea of these by riding along the brink, and looking down at various points on the sublime expanse. Nevertheless, a descent into the Cañon is essential for a proper estimate of its details, and one can never realize the enormity of certain cliffs and the extent of certain valleys, till he has crawled like a maimed insect at their base and looked thence upward to the narrowed sky. Yet such an investigation of the Cañon is, after all, merely like going down from a balloon into a great city to examine one of its myriad streets, since any gorge we may select for our descending path is but a tiny section of a laby-

ON HANCE'S TRAIL.

SECTION OF THE COLORADO RIVER IN THE CAÑON.

A VISION OF SUBLIMITY.

rinth. That which is unique and incomparable here is the view from the brink; and when the promised hotel is built upon the border of the Cañon, visitors will be content to remain for days at their windows or on the piazzas, feasting their souls upon a scene always sublime and sometimes terrible.

Nevertheless, desirous of exploring a specimen of these chasms (as we often select for minute examination a single painting out of an entire picture gallery) we made the descent to the Colorado by means of a crooked scratch upon a mountain side, which one might fancy had been blazed by a zigzag flash of lightning. As it requires four hours to wriggle down this path, and an equal amount of time to wriggle up, I spent the greater part of a day on what a comrade humorously styled the "quarter-deck of a mule." A square, legitimate seat

STARTING DOWN THE TRAIL.

in the saddle was usually impossible, so steep was the incline; and hence, when going down, I braced my feet and lay back on the haunches of the beast, and, in coming up, had to lean forward and clutch the pommel, to keep from sliding off, as a human avalanche, on the head of the next in line. In many places, however, riding was impossible, and we were compelled to scramble over the rocks on foot. The effect of hours of this exercise on muscles unaccustomed to such surprises may be imagined; yet, owing to the wonderfully restorative air of Arizona, the next day after this, the severest physical exertion I had ever known, I did not feel the slightest bad result, and was as fresh as ever. That there is an element of danger in this trip cannot be doubted. At times the little trail, on which two mules could not possibly have passed each other, skirts a precipice where the least misstep would hurl the traveler to destruction; and every turn of the zigzag path is so sharp that first the head and then the tail of the mule inevitably projects above the abyss, and wigwags to the mule below. Moreover, though not a vestige of a parapet consoles the dizzy rider, in several places the animal simply puts its feet together and toboggans down the smooth face of a slanting rock, bringing up at the bottom with a jerk that makes the tourist see a large variety of constellations, and even causes his beast to belch forth an involuntary roar of disenchantment, or else to try to pulverize his immediate successor. In such a place as this Nature seems pitiless and cruel; and one is impressed with the reflection that a million lives might be crushed out in any section of this maze of gorges and not a feature of it would be changed. There is, however, a fascination in gambling with danger, when a desirable prize is to be gained. The stake we risk may be our lives, yet, when the chances are in our favor, we often love to match excitement against the possibility of death; and even at the end, when we are safe, a sigh sometimes escapes us, as when the curtain falls on an absorbing play.

A YAWNING CHASM.

OBLIGED TO WALK.

As we descended, it grew warmer, not only from the greater elevation of the sun at noon, but from the fact that in this sudden drop of six thousand feet we had passed through several zones of temperature. Snow, for example, may be covering the summits of the mountains in midwinter, while at the bottom of the Cañon are summer warmth and vernal flowers. When, after two or three hours of continuous descent, we looked back at our starting-point, it seemed incredible that we had ever stood upon the pinnacles that towered so far above us, and were apparently piercing the slowly moving clouds. The effect was that of looking up from the bottom of a gigantic well. Instinctively I asked myself if I should ever return to that distant upper world, and it gave me a memorable realization of my individual insignificance to stand in such a sunken solitude, and realize that the fissure I was exploring was only a single loop in a vast network of ravines, which, if extended in a straight line, would make a cañon seven hundred miles in length. It was with relief that we reached, at last, the terminus of the lateral ravine we had been following and at the very bottom of the Cañon rested on the bank of the Colorado. The river is a little freer here than elsewhere in its tortuous course, and for some hundred feet is less compressed by the grim granite cliffs which, usually, rise in smooth black walls hundreds of feet in almost vertical height, and for two hundred miles retain in their embrace the restless, foaming flood that has no other avenue of escape.

The navigation of this river by Major J. W. Powell, in 1869, was one of the most daring deeds of exploration ever achieved by man, and the thrilling story of his journey down the Colorado, for more than a thousand miles, and through the entire length of the Grand Cañon, is as exciting as the most sensational romance. Despite the remonstrances of friends and the warnings of friendly Indians, Major Powell, with a flotilla of four boats and nine men, started down the river, on May 24th, from Green River City, in Utah, and, on the 30th of August, had completed his stupendous task, with the loss of two

A CABIN ON THE TRAIL.

A HALT.

boats and four men. Of the latter, one had deserted at an early date and escaped; but the remaining three, unwilling to brave any longer the terrors of the unknown Cañon, abandoned the expedition and tried to return through the desert, but were massacred by Indians. It is only when one stands beside a portion of this lonely river, and sees it shooting stealthily and swiftly from a rift in the Titanic cliffs and disappearing mysteriously between dark gates of granite, that he realizes what a heroic exploit the first navigation of this river was; for nothing had been known of its imprisoned course through this entanglement of chasms, or could be known, save by ex-

AT THE BOTTOM.

ploring it in boats, so difficult of access were, and are, the two or three points where it is possible for a human being to reach its perpendicular banks. Accordingly, when the valiant navigators sailed into these mysterious waters, they knew that there was almost every chance against the possibility of a boat's living in such a seething current, which is, at intervals, punctured with a multitude of tusk-like rocks, tortured into rapids, twisted into whirlpools, or broken by falls; while in the event of shipwreck they could hope for little save naked precipices to cling to for support. Moreover, after a heavy rain the Colorado often rises here fifty or sixty feet under the veritable cataracts of water which, for miles, stream directly down the perpendicular walls, and make of it a maddened torrent wilder than the rapids of Niagara. All honor, then, to Powell and his comrades who braved not alone the actual dangers thus described, but stood continually alert for unknown perils, which any bend in the swift, snake-like river might disclose, and which would make the gloomy groove through which they slipped a black-walled *oubliette*, or gate to Acheron.

TAKING LUNCH NEAR THE RIVER.

BESIDE THE COLORADO.

If any river in the world should be regarded with superstitious reverence, it is the Colorado, for it represents to us, albeit in a diminished form, the element that has produced the miracle of the Arizona Cañon, — water. Far back in the distant Eocene Epoch of our planet's history, the Colorado was the outlet of an inland sea which drained off toward the

Pacific, as the country of northwestern Arizona rose; and the Grand Cañon illustrates, on a stupendous scale, the system of erosion which, in a lesser degree, has deeply furrowed the entire region. At first one likes to think of the excavation of this awful chasm as the result of some tremendous cataclysm of Nature; but, in reality, it has all been done by water, assisted, no doubt, by the subtler action of the winds and storms in the disintegration of the

MONSTER CLIFFS, AND A NOTCH IN THE CAÑON WALL.

MILES OF I

monster cliffs, which, as they slowly crumbled into dust, were carried downward by the rains, and, finally, were borne off by the omnivorous river to the sea.

But though, at first, these agents do not seem as forceful and extraordinary as a single terrible catastrophe, the slow results thus gained are even more impressive. For what an appalling lapse of time must have been necessary to cut down and remove layers of sandstone, marble, and granite, thousands of feet in thickness; to carve the mighty shrines of Siva and of Vishnu, and to etch out these scores of interlacing cañons! To calculate it one must reckon a century for every turn of the hourglass. It is the story of a struggle maintained for ages between the solid and the fluid elements, in which at last the yielding water won a victory over adamant. It is an evidence, too, of Nature's patient methods; a triumph of the delicate over the strong, the liquid over the solid, the transitory over the enduring. At present, the softer material has been exhausted, and the rapacious river, shrunken in size, must satisfy itself by gnawing only the archaic granite which still curbs its course.

NG CAÑONS.

Yet if this calculation overpowers us, what shall we say of the reflections awakened by the fact that all the limestone cliffs along the lofty edges of the Cañon are composed of fossils,— the skeletons of creatures that once lived here covered by an ocean, and that ten thousand feet of strata, which formerly towered above the present summits of the Cañon walls, have been eroded and swept downward to the sea! Hence, were the missing strata (all of which are found in regular sequence in the high plateaus of Utah) restored, this Cañon would be sixteen thousand feet in depth, and from its borders one could look down upon a mountain higher than Mont Blanc! To calculate the æons implied in the repeated elevations and subsidences which made this region what it is would be almost to comprehend eternity. In such a retrospect centuries crumble and disappear into the gulf of Time as pebbles into the Cañon of the Colorado.

On my last evening in the pine tree camp I left my tent and walked alone to the edge of the Grand Cañon. The night was white with the splendor of the moon. A shimmering lake of silvery vapor rolled its noiseless tide against the mountains, and laved the terraces of the Hindu shrines. The lunar radiance, falling into such profundity, was powerless to reveal the plexus of subordinate cañons, and even the temples glimmered through the upper air like wraiths of the huge forms which they reveal by day. Advancing cautiously to an isolated point upon the brink, I lay upon my face, and peered down into the spectral void. No voice of man, nor cry of bird, nor roar of beast resounded through those awful corridors of silence. Even thought had no existence in that sunken realm of chaos. I felt as if I were the sole survivor of the deluge. Only the melancholy murmur of the wind ascended from that sepulchre of centuries. It seemed the requiem for a vanished world.

YELLOWSTONE NATIONAL PARK

THE ROAD NEAR THE GOLDEN GATE.

YELLOWSTONE NATIONAL PARK

ON certain portions of our globe Almighty God has set a special imprint of divinity. The Alps, the Pyrénées, the Mexican volcanoes, the solemn grandeur of Norwegian fjords, the sacred Mountain of Japan, and the sublimity of India's Himalayas — at different epochs in a life of travel — have filled my soul with awe and admiration. But now there ranks with these forevermore in my remembrance the country of the Yellowstone. Two-thirds across this continent, hidden away in the heart of the Rocky Mountains, eight thousand feet above the

LONE STAR GEYSER.

THE GROTTO, GEYSER'S CONE.

level of the sea, there lies a marvelous section of our earth, about one-half as large as the State of Connecticut. On three sides this is guarded by lofty, well-nigh inaccessible mountains, as though the Infinite Himself would not allow mankind to rashly enter its sublime enclosure. In this respect our Government has wisely imitated the Creator. It has proclaimed to all the world the sanctity of this peculiar area. It has received it as a gift from God and, as His trustee, holds it for the welfare of humanity. We, then, as citizens of the United States, are its possessors and its guardians. It is our National Park. Yet, although easy of access, most of us let the years go by without exploring it! How little we realize what a treasure we possess is proven by the fact that, until recently, the majority of tourists here were foreigners! I thought my previous store of memories was rich, but to have added to it the recollections of the Yellowstone will give a greater happiness to life while life shall last. Day after day, yes, hour after hour, within the girdle of its snow-capped peaks I looked upon a constant series of stupendous sights — a blending of the beautiful and terrible, the strange and the sublime — which were, moreover, so peculiar that they stand out distinct and different from those of every other portion of our earth.

To call our National Park the "Switzerland of America" would be absurd. It is not Switzerland; it is not Iceland; it is not Norway; it is unique; and the unique cannot be compared. If I were asked to describe it in a dozen lines, I should call it the arena of an enormous amphitheatre. Its architect was Nature; the gladiators that contended in it were volcanoes. During unnumbered ages those gladiators struggled to surpass one another in destruction by pouring forth great floods of molten lava. Even now the force which animated them still shows itself in other forms, but harmlessly, much as a captive serpent hisses though its fangs are drawn.

ENTRANCE TO THE PARK.

But the volcanoes give no sign of life. They are dead actors in a fearful tragedy performed here countless centuries before the advent of mankind, with this entire region for a stage, and for their only audience the sun and stars.

I shall never forget our entrance into this theatre of sublime phenomena. The Pullman car, in which we had taken our places at St. Paul, had carried us in safety more than a thousand miles and had left us at the gateway of the park. Before us was a portion of the road, eight miles in length, which leads the tourist to the Mammoth Springs Hotel. On one side an impetuous river shouted a welcome as we rode along. Above us rose gray, desolate cliffs. They are volcanic in their origin. The brand of fire is on them all. They are symbolic, therefore, of the entire park; for fire and water are the two great forces here which have, for ages, struggled for supremacy.

THE WATCHFUL SENTINEL.

THE MAMMOTH SPRINGS HOTEL.

No human being dwells upon those dreary crags, but at one point, as I looked up at them, I saw — poised statue-like above a mighty pinnacle of rock — a solitary eagle. Pausing, with outstretched wings above its nest, it seemed to look disdainfully upon us human pygmies crawling far below. Living at such a height, in voluntary isolation, that king of birds appeared the very embodiment of strength and majesty. Call it a touch of superstition, if you will, yet I confess it thrilled me to the heart to find that here, above the very entrance to the Wonderland of our Republic, there should be stationed midway between earth and heaven, like a watchful sentinel, our national bird, — the bird of freedom!

At length a sudden turn revealed to us our first halting-place within the Park, — the Mammoth Springs Hotel. The structure in itself looked mammoth as we approached it, for its portico exceeds four hundred feet in length. Our first

HALL OF THE MAMMOTH SPRINGS HOTEL.

impressions were agreeable. Porters rushed forth and helped us to alight, and on the broad piazza the manager received us cordially. Everything had the air of an established summer resort. This, I confess, surprised me greatly, as I had expected primitive accommodations, and supposed that, though the days of camping-out had largely passed away, the resting-places in the Park were still so crude that one would be glad to leave them. But I lingered here with pleasure long after all the wonders of the Park had been beheld. The furniture, though simple, is sufficient; to satisfy our national nervousness, the halls are so well-stocked with rocking-chairs that European visitors look about

THE PHOTOGRAPHER'S HOUSE.

MAMMOTH HOT SPRINGS.

them with alarm, and try to find some seats that promise a more stable equilibrium; the sleeping-rooms are scrupulously clean; soft blankets, snow-white sheets, and comfortable beds assure a good night's rest; and the staff of colored waiters in the dining-room, steam-heat, a bell-boy service, and electric lights made us forget our distance from great cities and the haunts of men. Moreover, what is true of this is true, as well, of the other hotels within the Park; and when I add that well-cooked food is served in all of them, it will be seen that tourists need not fear a lengthy sojourn in these hostelries.

Standing on the veranda of the Mammoth Hot Springs Hotel, I saw between me and the range of mountains opposite a broad plateau, on which were grouped a dozen neat and tasteful structures. With the exception of the photographer's house in the foreground, these constitute Fort Yellowstone. "A fort!" the visitor exclaims, "impossible! These buildings are of wood, not stone. Where are its turrets, battlements, and guns?" Nevertheless, this is a station for two companies of United States Cavalry; most of the houses being resi-

FORT YELLOWSTONE.

A FOREST IN THE PARK.

dences for the officers, while in the rear are barracks for the soldiers.

No one who has visited the National Park ever doubts the necessity of having soldiers there. Thus, one of the most important duties of the United States troops, stationed within its area, is to save its splendid forests from destruction. To do this calls for constant vigilance. A fire started in the resinous pines, which cover many of the mountain sides, leaps forward with such fury that it would overtake a horseman fleeing for his life. To guard against so serious a calamity, soldiers patrol the Park continually to see that all the camp-fires have been extinguished. Thanks to their watchful care, only one notable conflagration has occurred here in the last eight years, and that the soldiers fought with energy for twenty days, till the last vestige of it was subdued.

The tourist comprehends the great importance of this work

when he beholds the rivers of the Park threading, like avenues of silver, the sombre frame-work of the trees, and recollects that just such forests as adjoin these streams cover no less than eighty-four per cent. of its entire area. In a treeless country like Wyoming these forests are of priceless value, because of their utility in holding back, in spring, the melting snow. Some of the largest rivers of our continent are fed from the well-timbered area of the Yellowstone; and if the trees were destroyed, the enormous snowfall in the Park, unsheltered from the sun, would melt so rapidly that the swollen torrents would quickly wash away roads, bridges, and productive farms, even, far out in the adjacent country, and, subsequently, cause a serious drought for many months.

Another very important labor of the United States soldiers here is to preserve the game within the Park. It is the purpose of our Government to make this area a place of refuge for those animals which man's insatiate greed has now almost destroyed. The remoteness of this lofty region, together with its mountain fastnesses, deep forests, and sequestered glens, makes

FIRE-HOLE RIVER.

MOUNTAIN SHEEP.

it an almost perfect game-preserve. There are at present thirty thousand elk within the Park; its deer and antelopes are steadily increasing; and bears, foxes, and small game roam unmolested here. Buffaloes, however, are still few in number. They have become too valuable. A buffalo head, which formerly could be bought for a mere trifle, commands, to-day, a price of five hundred dollars. Hence, daring poachers sometimes run the risk of entering the Park in winter and destroying them.

It is sad to reflect how the buffaloes of this continent have been almost exterminated. As late as thirty years ago, trains often had to halt upon the prairies; and even steamboats were, occasionally, obliged to wait an hour or two in the Missouri River until enormous herds of buffalo had crossed their path. Now only about two hundred of these animals are in existence, — the sole survivors of the millions that once thundered over the western plains, and disputed with the Indians the ownership of this great continent.

YELLOWSTONE ELK.

Until very recently, travelers on our prairies frequently beheld the melancholy sight of laborers gathering up the buffalo

BUFFALOES IN THE SNOW.

bones which lay upon the plains, like wreckage floating on the sea. Hundreds of carloads of these skeletons were shipped to factories in the east. Now, to protect the few remaining buffaloes, as well as other animals, our troops patrol the Park even in winter. The principal stations are connected by telephone, and information given thus is promptly acted on. No traveler is allowed to carry fire-arms; and any one who attempts to destroy animal life is liable to a fine of one thousand dollars, or imprisonment for two years, or both.

GATHERING BUFFALO BONES.

Still another task, devolving upon the Military Governor of the Park, is the building and repairing of its roads. No doubt the Superintendent is doing all he can with the amount of money that the Government allows him; but there is room for great improvement in these thoroughfares, if Congress will but make a suitable appropriation for the purpose. At present, a part of the coaching-route is of necessity traveled over twice. This should be obviated by constructing one more road, by which the tourist could be brought to several interesting features of the Park that are now rarely seen.

Every one knows how roads in Europe climb the steepest grades in easy curves, and are usually as smooth as a marble table, free from obstacles, and carefully walled-in by parapets of stone. Why should not we possess such roads, especially in our National Park? Dust is at present a great drawback to the traveler's pleasure here; but this could be prevented if the roads were thoroughly macadamized. Surely, the honor of our Government demands that this unique museum of marvels should be the pride and glory of the nation, with highways equal to any in the world.

Only a few hundred feet distant from the Mammoth Springs

A YELLOWSTONE ROAD.

LIBERTY CAP.

Hotel stands a strange, naturally molded shaft of stone, fifty-two feet in height. From certain points its summit calls to mind the head-dress of the Revolution, and hence its name is Liberty Cap. It is a fitting monument to mark the entrance into Wonderland, for it is the cone of an old geyser long since dead. Within it is a tube of unknown depth. Through that, ages since, was hurled at intervals a stream of boiling water, precisely as it comes from active geysers in the Park to-day. But now the hand of Time has stilled its passionate pulsations, and laid upon its stony lips the seal of silence. At only a little distance from this eloquent reminder of the past I peered into a cavern hundreds of feet deep. It was once the reservoir of a geyser. An atmosphere of sulphur haunts it still. No doubt this whole plateau is but the cover of extinguished fires, for other similar caves pierce the locality on which the hotel stands. A feeling of solemnity stole over me as I surveyed these dead or dying agents of volcanic power. In the great battle of the

A MOUND OF THE HOT SPRING TERRACES.

elements, which has been going on here for unnumbered centuries, they doubtless took an active part. But Time has given them a mortal wound; and now they are waiting patiently until their younger comrades, farther up the Park, shall, one by one, like them grow cold and motionless.

Not more than fifty feet from Liberty Cap rise the famous Hot Spring Terraces. They constitute a veritable mountain, covering at least two hundred acres, the whole of which has been, for centuries, growing slowly through the agency of hot water issuing from the boiling springs. This, as it cools, leaves a mineral deposit, spread out in delicate, thin layers by the soft ripples of the heated flood. Strange, is it not? Everywhere else the flow of water wears away the substance that it touches; but here, by its peculiar sediment, it builds as surely as the coral insect. Moreover, the coloring of these terraces is, if possible, even more marvelous than their creation; for, as the mineral water pulsates over them, it forms a great variety of brilliant hues. Hot water, therefore, is to this material what blood is to the body. With it the features glow with warmth and color; without it they are cold and ghostlike. Accordingly, where water ripples over these gigantic steps, towering one above another toward the sky, they look like beautiful cascades of color; and when the liquid has deserted them, they stand out like a staircase of Carrara marble. Hence, through the changing centuries, they pass in slow succession, from light to shade, from brilliancy to pallor, and from life to death. This mineral water is not only a mysterious architect; it is, also, an artist that no man can equal. Its magic touch has intermingled the finest shades of orange, yellow, purple, red, and brown; sometimes in solid masses, at other places diversified by slender threads, like skeins of multicolored silk. Yet in producing all these wonderful effects, there is no violence, no uproar. The boiling water passes over the mounds it has produced with the low murmur of a sweet cascade. Its tiny wavelets

MINERVA TERRACE.

touch the stone work like a sculptor's fingers, molding the yielding mass into exquisitely graceful forms.

The top of each of these colored steps is a pool of boiling water. Each of these tiny lakes is radiant with lovely hues, and is bordered by a colored coping, resembling a curb of jasper or of porphyry. Yet the thinnest knife-blade can be placed here on the dividing line between vitality and death. The contrast is as sudden and complete as that between the desert and the valley of the Nile. Where Egypt's river ends its overflow the desert sands begin; and on these terraces it is the same. Where the life-giving water fails, the golden colors become ashen. This terraced mountain, therefore, seemed to me like a colossal checker-board, upon whose colored squares, the two great forces, Life and Death, were playing their eternal game. There is a pathos in this evanescent beauty. What lies about us in one place so gray and ghostly was once as bright and beautiful as that which we perceive a hun-

JUPITER TERRACE.

"VITALITY AND DEATH."

dred feet away. But nothing here retains supremacy. The glory of this century will be the gravestone of the next. Around our feet are sepulchres of vanished splendor. It seems as if the architect were constantly dissatisfied. No sooner has he finished one magnificent structure than he impatiently begins another, leaving the first to crumble and decay. Each new production seems to him the finest; but never reaching his ideal, he speedily abandons it to perish from neglect.

It cannot be said of these terraces that "distance lends enchantment to the view." The nearer you come to them the more beautiful they appear. They even bear the inspection of a magnifying glass, for they are covered with a bead-like ornamentation worthy of the goldsmith's art. In one place, for example, rise pulpits finer than those of Pisa or Siena. Their edges seem to be of purest jasper. They are upheld by tapering shafts resembling richly decorated organ-pipes. From parapets of porphyry hang gold stalactites, side by side with

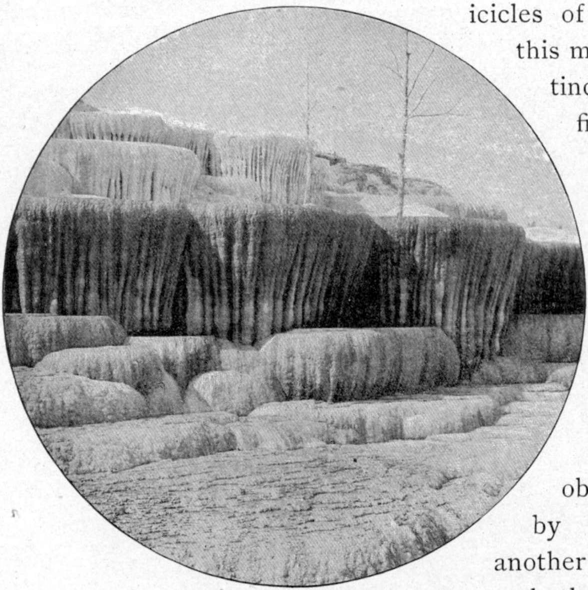

"SEPULCHRES OF VANISHED SPLENDOR."

icicles of silver. Moreover, all this marvelous fretwork is distinctly visible, for the light film of water pulsates over it so delicately that it can no more hide the filigree beneath than a thin veil conceals a face.

It is a melancholy fact that were it not for United States troops, these beautiful objects would be mutilated by relic-hunters. Hence, another duty of our soldiers is to watch the formations constantly, lest tourists should break off specimens, and ruin them forever, and lest still more ignoble vandals, whose fingers itch for notoriety, should write upon these glorious works of nature their worthless names, and those of the towns unfortunate enough to have produced them. All possible measures are taken to prevent this vandalism. Thus, every tourist entering the Park must register his name. Most travelers do so, as a matter of course, at the hotels, but even the arrivals of those who come here

MAN AND NATURE.

THE PULPIT TERRACE.

to camp must be duly recorded at the Superintendent's office. If a soldier sees a name, or even initials, written on the stone, he telephones the fact to the Military Governor. At once the lists are scanned for such a name. If found, the Superintendent wires an order to have the man arrested, and so careful is the search for all defacers, that the offending party is, usually, found before he leaves the Park. Then the Superintendent, like the Mikado, makes the punishment fit the crime. A scrubbing brush and laundry soap are given to the desecrator, and he is made to go back, perhaps forty miles or more, and with his own hands wash away the proofs of his disgraceful vanity. Not long ago a young man was arrested at six o'clock in the morning, made to leave his bed, and march without his breakfast several miles, to prove that he could be as skillful with a brush as with a pencil.

A CAMPING-PARTY.

After spending several days at the Mammoth Hot Springs, we started out to explore the greater marvels that awaited us in the interior. The mode of travel through the Park is a succession of coaching-parties over a distance of one hundred and eighty miles. The larger vehicles are drawn by six, the smaller ones by four, strong horses, well fed, well groomed, high spirited, yet safe. This feature of our National Park astonished me. I had formed no idea of its perfection or its magnitude. Here, for example, are vehicles enough to

A COACHING-PARTY.

accommodate seven hundred tourists for a continuous journey of five days! Here, too, are five hundred horses, all of which can be harnessed at twenty-four hours' notice; and, since the Park is so remote, here also are the company's blacksmith and repair shops. Within the stables, also, are the beautifully varnished coaches, varying in cost from one to two thousand dollars, and made in Concord, New Hampshire, twenty-five hundred miles away. On one of these I read the number, "$13\frac{1}{2}$." "Why did you add the fraction?" I inquired of the Manager of Transportation. "Because," he replied, "some travelers would not take a

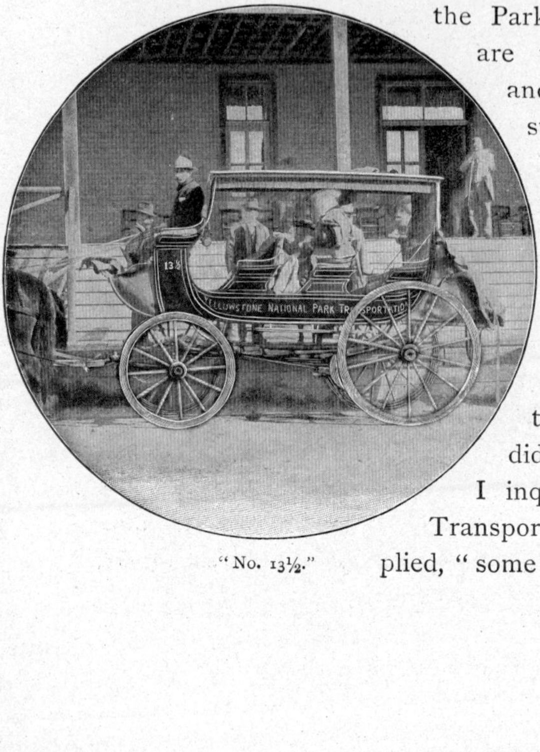

"No. 13½."

number thirteen coach. They feared a breakdown or a tumble into the river; so I put on the half to take ill-luck away." I dwell at length upon these practical details, because I have found that people, in general, do not know them. Most Americans have little idea whether the driving distance in the Park is ten miles, or a hundred. Especially are they ignorant of the fact that they may leave the coaches at any point, remain at a hotel as long as they desire, and then resume their journey

HOTEL AT YELLOWSTONE LAKE.

in other vehicles, without the least additional expense for transportation, precisely as one uses a stop-over ticket on a railroad.

The fact that it is possible to go through the Park in four or five days is not a reason why it is best to do so. Hundreds of tourists make the trip three times as rapidly as they would were they aware that they could remain comfortably for months. When this is better known, people will travel here more leisurely. Even now, parents with little children sometimes leave them at the Mammoth Springs Hotel in charge of nurses, and receive messages by telephone every day to inform them how they are. An important consideration, also, for invalids is the fact that two skilled surgeons, attendant on the army, are always easily accessible. Moreover, the

THE GOLDEN GATE.

climate of the Park in summer is delightful. It is true, the sun beats down at noonday fiercely, the thin air offering scant resistance to its rays, but in the shade one feels no heat at all. Light overcoats are needed when the sun goes down. There is scarcely a night here, through the year, which passes without frost. To me the pure dry air of that great height was more invigorating than any I had ever breathed, save, possibly, that of Norway, and it is, probably, the tonic of the atmosphere that renders even the invalid and agèd able to support long journeys in the Park without exhaustion. In all these years no tourist has been made ill here by fatigue.

A few miles after leaving the Hot Springs, we reached the entrance to a picturesque ravine, the tawny color of whose rocks has given it the name of Golden Gate. This is, alike, the entrance to, and exit from, the inner sanctuary of this land of marvels. Accordingly a solitary boulder, detached from its companions on the cliff, seems to be stationed at this portal like a sentinel to watch all tourists who come and go. At all events it echoes to the voices of those who enter almost as eager as seekers after gold; and, a week later, sees them return, browned by the sun, invigorated by the air, and joyful in the acquisition of incomparable memories.

Emerging from this Golden Gate, I looked about me with surprise, as the narrow walls of the ravine gave place to a plateau surrounded everywhere by snow-capped mountains, from

THE GOLDEN GATE, LOOKING OUTWARD.

which the Indians believed one could obtain a view of Paradise. Across this area, like a railroad traversing a prairie, stretched the driveway for our carriages.

"Do tourists usually seem delighted with the park?" I asked our driver.

"Invariably," he replied. "Of course I cannot understand the words of the foreigners, but their excited exclamations show their great enthusiasm. I like the tourists," he continued, "they are so grateful for any little favor! One of them said to me the other day, 'Is the water here good to drink?' 'Not always,' I replied, 'you must be careful.' At once he pressed my hand, pulled out a flask, and said, 'I thank you!'"

While crossing the plateau we enjoyed an admirable view of

THE PLATEAU.

ELECTRIC PEAK.

THE GLASS MOUNTAIN.

the loftiest of the mountains which form, around the Park, a rampart of protection. Its sharply pointed summit pierces the transparent air more than eleven thousand feet above the sea, and it is well named Electric Peak, since it appears to be a storage battery for all of the Rocky Mountains. Such are the mineral deposits on its sides, that the best instruments of engineers are thrown into confusion, and rendered useless, while the lightning on this favorite home of electricity is said to be unparalleled.

Presently a turn in the road revealed to us a dark-hued mountain rising almost perpendicularly from a lake. Marvelous to relate, the material of which this mountain is composed is jet-black glass, produced by volcanic fires. The very road on which we drove between this and the lake also consists of glass too hard to break beneath the wheels. The first explorers found this obsidian cliff almost impassable; but when they ascertained of what it was composed, they piled up timber at its base, and set it on fire. When the glass was hot, they dashed upon the heated mass cold water, which broke it into fragments. Then

AN INDIAN CHIEF.

with huge levers, picks, and shovels, they pushed and pried the shining pieces down into the lake, and opened thus a wagon-road a thousand feet in length.

The region of the Yellowstone was to most Indian tribes a place of horror. They trembled at the awful sights they here beheld. But the obsidian cliff was precious to them all. Its substance was as hard as flint, and hence well suited for their arrow-heads. This mountain of volcanic glass was, therefore, the great Indian armory; and as such it was neutral ground. Hither all hostile tribes might come for implements of war and then depart unharmed. While they were here a sacred, inter-tribal oath protected them. An hour later, those very warriors might meet in deadly combat, and turn against each other's breasts the weapons taken from that laboratory of an unknown power.

Can we wonder that, in former times, when all this region was still unexplored, and its majestic streams rolled nameless through a trackless wilderness, the statements of the few brave men who ventured into this enclosure were disbelieved by all who heard them? One old trapper became so angry when his stories of the place were doubted, that he deliberately revenged himself by inventing tales of which Münchhausen would have been proud. Thus, he declared, that one day when he was hunting here he saw a bear. He fired at it, but without result. The animal did not even notice him. He fired again, yet the big bear kept on graz-

A TRAPPER.

ing. The hunter in astonishment then ran forward, but suddenly dashed against a solid mountain made of glass. Through that, he said, he had been looking at the animal. Unspeakably amazed, he finally walked around the mountain, and was just taking aim again, when he discovered that the glass had acted like a telescope, and that the bear was twenty-five miles away!

Not far from the volcanic cliff which gave the trapper inspiration for his story, we reached one of the most famous basins of the Park. In briefest terms, these basins are the

THE NORRIS BASIN.

spots in the arena where the crust is thinnest. They are the trap-doors in a volcanic stage through which the fiery actors in the tragedy of Nature, which is here enacted, come upon the scene. Literally, they are the vents through which the steam and boiling water can escape. In doing so, however, the water, as at the Mammoth Springs, leaves a sediment of pure white lime or silica. Hence, from a distance, these basins look like desolate expanses of white sand. Beside them always flows a river which carries off the boiling water to the outer world.

A PLACE OF DANGER.

No illustration can do justice to what is called the Norris Basin, but it is horrible enough to test the strongest nerves. Having full confidence in our guide (the Park photographer) we ventured with him, outside the usual track of tourists, and went where all the money of the Rothschilds would not have tempted us to go alone. The crust beneath our feet was hot, and often quivered as we walked. A single misstep to the right or left would have been followed by appalling consequences. Thus, a careless soldier, only a few days before, had broken through, and was then lying in the hospital with both legs badly scalded. Around us were a hundred vats of water, boiling furiously; the air was heavy with the fumes of sulphur; and the whole expanse was seamed with cracks and honeycombed with holes from which a noxious vapor crept out to pollute the air. I thought of Dante's walk through hell, and called to mind the burning lake, which he describes, from which the wretched sufferers vainly sought to free themselves.

Leaving, at last, this roof of the infernal regions, just as we again stood apparently on solid ground, a fierce explosion close

A CAMPING-STATION.

beside us caused us to start and run for twenty feet. Our guide laughed heartily. "Come back," he said, "don't be afraid. It is only a baby geyser, five years old." In fact, in 1891, a sudden outburst of volcanic fury made an opening here, through which, at intervals of thirty minutes, day and night, hot water now leaps forth in wild confusion.

"This, then, is a geyser!" I exclaimed.

"Bah!" said the guide, contemptuously, "if you had seen the real geysers in the Upper Basin, you would not look at this."

Meantime, for half an hour we had been hearing, more and more distinctly, a dull, persistent roar, like the escape of steam from a transatlantic liner. At last we reached the cause. It is a mass of steam which rushes from an opening in the ground, summer and winter, year by year, in one unbroken volume. The rock around it is as black as jet; hence it is called the Black Growler. Think of the awful power confined beneath the

A BABY GEYSER.

surface here, when this one angry voice can be distinctly heard four miles away. Choke up that aperture, and what a terrible convulsion would ensue, as the accumulated steam burst its prison walls! It is a sight which makes one long to lift the cover from this monstrous caldron, learn the cause of its stupendous heat, and trace the complicated and mysterious aqueducts through which the steam and water make their way.

THE BLACK GROWLER

Returning from the Black Growler, we halted at a lunch-station, the manager of which is Larry. All visitors to the Park remember Larry. He has a different welcome for each guest: "Good-day, Professor. Come in, my Lord. The top of the morning to you, Doctor." These phrases flow as lightly from his tongue as water from a geyser. His station is a mere tent; but he will say, with most amusing seriousness: "Gintlemen, walk one flight up and turn to the right. Ladies, come

LARRY.

this way and take the elevator. Now thin, luncheon is ready. Each guest take one seat, and as much food as he can get."

"Where did you come from, Larry?" I asked.

"From Brooklyn, Sor," was his reply, "but I'll niver go back there, for all my friends have been killed by the trolley cars."

Larry is very democratic. The other day a guest, on sitting down to lunch, took too much room upon the bench. "Plaze move along, Sor," said Larry.

The stranger glared at him. "I am a Count," he remarked at last.

"Well, Sor," said Larry, "here you only count wun!"

"Hush!" exclaimed a member of the gentleman's suite, "that is Count Schouvaloff."

"I'll forgive him that," said Larry, "if he won't shuffle off this seat." Pointing to my companion, Larry asked me: "What is that gintleman's business?"

"He is a teacher of singing," I answered.

"Faith," said Larry, "I'd like to have him try my voice. There is something very strange about my

LARRY'S LUNCH-STATION.

THE BISCUIT BASIN.

vocal chords. Whenever I sing, the Black Growler stops. One tourist told me it was a case of professional jealousy, and said the Black Growler was envious of my *forte* tones. 'I have not forty tones,' I said, 'I've only one tone.' 'Well,' says he, 'make a note of it!'"

Only once in his life has Larry been put to silence. Two years ago, a gentleman remarked to him: "Well, Larry, good-by; come and visit me next winter in the East. In my house you shall have a nice room, and, if you are ill, shall enjoy a doctor's services free of all expense."

"Thank you," said Larry, "plaze give me your card."

The tourist handed it to him; and Larry, with astonishment and horror, read beneath the gentleman's name these words: "Superintendent of the Insane Asylum, Utica, New York."

Some hours after leaving Larry's lunch-station, we reached another area of volcanic action. Our nerves were steadier now. The close proximity to Hades was less evident; yet here hot mineral water had spread broadcast innumerable little mounds of silica, which look so much like biscuits grouped in a colossal pan that this is called the Biscuit Basin; but they are not the kind that "mother used to make." If a tourist asked for bread here, he would receive a stone; since all these so-called biscuits are as hard as flint. We walked upon their crusts with perfect safety; yet, in so doing, our boots grew warm beneath our feet, for the water in this miniature archipelago is heated to the boiling point.

"Show me a geyser!" I at last exclaimed impatiently, "I want to see a genuine geyser." Accordingly our guide conducted us to what he announced as "The Fountain." I looked around me with surprise. I saw no fountain, but merely a pool of boiling water, from which the light breeze bore away a thin, transparent cloud of steam. It is true, around this was a pavement as delicately fashioned as any piece of coral ever

A GEYSER POOL.

taken from the sea. Nevertheless, while I admired that, I could not understand why this comparatively tranquil pool was called a geyser, and frankly said I was disappointed. But, even as I spoke, I saw to my astonishment the boiling water in this reservoir sink and disappear from view.

"Where has it gone?" I eagerly inquired.

"Stand back!" shouted the guide, "she's coming."

I ran back a few steps, then turned and caught my breath for at that very instant, up from the pool which I had just beheld so beautiful and tranquil, there rose in one great outburst of sublimity such a stupendous mass of water as I had never imagined possible in a vertical form. I knew that it was boiling, and that a deluge of those scalding drops would probably mean death, but I was powerless to move. Amazement and delight enchained me spellbound. Talk of a fountain! This was a cloud-burst of the rarest jewels which, till that moment, had been held in solution in a subterranean cavern, but which had suddenly crystallized into a million radiant forms on

"A CLOUD-BURST OF JEWELS."

THE OBLONG GEYSER.

thus emerging into light and air. The sun was shining through the glittering mass; and myriads of diamonds, moonstones, pearls, and opals mingled in splendid rivalry two hundred feet above our heads.

We soon approached another of the many geysers in the basin. They are all different. Around one, a number of colored blocks, exquisitely decorated by the geyser's waves, appeared to have been placed artistically in an oblong frame. When I first beheld them, they looked like huge sea-monsters which, startled by our footsteps, were about to plunge into the depths.

What is there in the natural world so fascinating and mysterious as a geyser? What, for example, is the depth of its intensely-colored pool of boiling water? No one can tell. One thing, however, is certain; the surface of the pool is but the summit of a liquid column. Its base is in a subterranean reservoir. Into that reservoir there flows a volume of cold water, furnished by the rain or snow, or by infiltration from some lake, or river. Meantime, the walls of the deep reservoir are heated by volcanic fire. Accordingly the water, in contact with these walls, soon begins to boil, and a great mass of steam collects above it. There must, of course, be some escape for this, and, finally, it makes its exit, hurling the boiling water to a height of one or two hundred feet, according to the force of the explosion. Imagine, then, the amount of water that even one such reservoir contains; for some of these volcanic fountains play for more than half an hour before their contents are discharged! Think, also, that in this basin there are no less than thirty geysers, seventeen of which have been observed in action simultaneously.

THE GIANT GEYSER.

THE CASTLE GEYSER.

Thus far we had seen merely geysers which arise from pools; but, presently, we approached one which in the course of ages has built up for itself a cone, or funnel, for its scalding waves.

"That," said our guide, "is the Castle Geyser."

"That rock a geyser!" I exclaimed incredulously, "it looks like an old ruin, without a single indication of activity; save, possibly, the little cloud of steam that hangs above it, as if it were the breath of some mysterious monster sleeping far below."

"If you doubt it," he replied, "go nearer and examine it."

We did so. I

ON "ITS FLINTY SIDES."

THE CASTLE GEYSER'S CONE.

scrambled up its flinty sides, and found an opening in the summit three feet wide. I touched the rock. It was still warm, and yet no water was discernible. No sound was audible within its depths.

"If this be really a geyser," I remarked, "it is no doubt a lifeless one like Liberty Cap."

My comrade smiled, looked at his watch, then at his note-book, and finally replied: "Wait half an hour and see."

Accordingly, we lingered on the massive ledges of the Castle Geyser, and learned that it is the largest, probably the oldest, of all the active geyser cones within the Park. Once its eruptions were no doubt stupendous; but now its power is waning. The gradual closing up of its huge throat, and the increasing substitution of steam for water, prove that the monster has now entered on the final stage of its career; for here, as on the terraces, we are surrounded by specimens of life, decay, and death. The young, the middle-agèd, the old, the dead, — they are all here!

The fiery agitation of the pool and the impulsive spurts of water are indicative of youth. A steady, splendid outburst proves maturity. The feebler action of the Castle shows the waning powers of old age. Last of all comes the closed cone, like a sealed sarcophagus, and that is death.

Meantime, the thirty minutes of expectancy had passed; and, suddenly, with a tremendous rush of steam, the Castle proved that its resources were by no means exhausted. At the same instant, half a mile away, the Beehive Geyser threw into the air a shaft of dazzling spray fully two hundred feet in height. I realized then, as never before, the noble action of our Government in giving this incomparable region to the people. If this had not been done, the selfishness and greed of man would have made a tour here almost unbearable. A fence would, doubtless, have been built around every geyser, and fees would have been charged to witness each wonderful phenomenon; whereas, to-day, thanks to the generosity of Congress, the Park itself, and everything that it contains, are

THE CASTLE AND THE BEEHIVE IN ACTION.

absolutely free to all, rich and poor, native and foreigner,—forever consecrated to the education and delight of man.

But no enumeration of the geysers would be complete without a mention of the special favorite of tourists, Old Faithful. The opening through which this miracle of Nature springs is at the summit of a beautifully ornamented mound, which is itself a page in Nature's wonder-book. The lines upon its wrinkled face tell of a past whose secrets still remain a mystery. It hints of an antiquity so vast that one contemplates it with bated breath; for this entire slope has been built up, atom after atom, through unnumbered ages; during which time, no doubt, the geyser hour by hour has faithfully performed its part, without an eye to note its splendor, or a voice to tell its glory to the world. Old Faithful does not owe its popularity entirely to height or beauty, though it possesses both. It is beloved for its fidelity. Whatever irregularities other geysers show, Old Faithful never fails. Year in, year out, winter and summer, day and night, in cold and

THE CRATER OF OLD FAITHFUL.

CASTLE AND OLD FAITHFUL GEYSERS.

heat, in sunshine and in storm, Old Faithful every seventy minutes sends up its silvery cascade to the height of about one hundred and eighty feet. Of all the geysers known to man this is the most reliable and perfect. Station yourself before it watch in hand and, punctual to the moment, it will never disappoint you. Few realize on how large a scale the forces of Nature work here. At each eruption, Old Faithful pours forth about one million five hundred thousand gallons, or more than thirty-three million gallons in one day! This geyser alone, therefore, could easily supply with water a city of the size of Boston.

OLD FAITHFUL IN ACTION.

Within this area of the active geysers is a place called Hell's Half Acre. It is rightly named. Rough, perpendicular ledges project over a monstrous gulf of unknown depth, from which great clouds of steam are constantly emerging. When the wind draws back for a moment a portion of this

HELL'S HALF ACRE.

sulphur-laden curtain, the visitor perceives a lake below, seething and boiling from internal heat. For years no one suspected this to be a geyser; but suddenly, in 1881, the underlying force hurled the entire lake up bodily to the height of two hundred and fifty feet, and even repeated the eruption frequently. After some months the exhibition ceased, and all was calm again for seven years. In 1888, however, it once more burst forth with prodigious energy, ejecting at each explosion more boiling water than all the other geysers in the Park combined. Even the surrounding ledges could not withstand this terrible upheaval, and tons of rock were sometimes thrown up, with the water, more than two hundred feet. It is not

THE EXCELSIOR, IN 1888.

strange, therefore, that this is called Excelsior, the King of Geysers. It is the most tremendous, awe-inspiring fountain in the world. When it will be again aroused, no one can tell. Its interval would seem to be from seven to ten years. Said an enthusiastic traveler to me: "If the Excelsior ever plays again, I will gladly travel three thousand miles to see it."

I have a vivid remembrance of my last night at the Upper

EVENING IN THE UPPER BASIN.

Basin. The hush of evening hallowed it. Alone and undisturbed we looked upon a scene unequaled in the world. Around us liquid columns rose and fell with ceaseless regularity. The cooler air of evening made many shafts of vapor visible which in the glare of day had vanished unperceived. So perfect were their images in the adjoining stream, that it was easy to believe the veil had been at last withdrawn, and that the hidden source of all this wonderful display had been

THE MORNING-GLORY POOL.

revealed. No sound from them was audible; no breeze disturbed their steadfast flight toward heaven; and in the deepening twilight, the slender, white-robed columns seemed like the ghosts of geysers, long since dead, revisiting the scenes of their activity.

But geysers do not constitute the only marvels of these volcanic basins. The beauty of their pools of boiling water is almost inconceivable to those who have not seen them. No illustration can do them justice; for no photographer can adequately reproduce their clear, transparent depths, nor can an artist's brush ever quite portray their peculiar coloring, due to the minerals held in solution, or else deposited upon their sides. I can deliberately say, however, that

PRISMATIC LAKE.

THE ROAD NEAR THE GOLDEN GATE.

some of the most exquisitely beautiful objects I have ever seen in any portion of the world are the superbly tinted caldrons of the Yellowstone.

Their hues are infinitely varied. Many are blue, some green, some golden, and some wine-colored, in all gradations of tone; and could we soar aloft and take of them a bird's-eye view, the glittering basin might seem to us a silver shield, studded with rubies, emeralds, turquoises, and sapphires. Moreover, these miniature lakes are lined with exquisite ornamentation. One sees in them, with absolute distinctness, a reproduction of the loveliest forms that he has ever found in floral or in vegetable life. Gardens of mushrooms, banks of goldenrod, or clusters of asparagus, appear to be growing here, created by the Architect and colored by the Artist of these mineral springs.

The most renowned of all these reservoirs of color is called the Emerald Pool. Painters from this and other lands have

THE EMERALD POOL.

tried repeatedly to depict this faithfully upon canvas, but, finally, have left it in despair. In fact, its coloring is so intense, that as the bubbles, rising to its surface, lift from this bowl their rounded forms, and pause a second in the air before they break, they are still just as richly tinted as the flood beneath. Accordingly this pool appeared to me like a colossal casket, filled with emeralds, which spirit hands from time to time drew gently upward from its jeweled depths.

Close by this is another boiling pool called the Sunlight Lake. On this I saw one of the most marvelous phenomena I have ever looked upon. The colors of this tiny sheet of water appeared not only in concentric circles, like the rings of a tree, but also in the order of the spectrum. The outer

SUNLIGHT LAKE.

THE DEVIL'S PUNCH-BOWL.

band was crimson, and then the unbroken sequence came: red, orange, yellow, green, blue, and violet in the centre! Moreover, the very steam arising from it (reflecting as it did the varied tints beneath) was exquisitely colored, and vanished into air like a dissolving rainbow. All these prismatic pools are clasped by beautifully decorated curbs of silica, and seem to be set in rings of gold, with mineral colors running through them like enamel. So delicate are the touches of the magic water, as the persistent heart-beats of old Mother Earth propel it over their ornamental rims, that every ripple leaves its tiny mark. Hence it is no exaggeration, but literal truth, to say that beautiful mosaic work is being formed each time the films of boiling water are dimpled by the passing breeze.

The great variety of wonders in our National Park was a continual source of pleasure and surprise to me. Thus, in the midst of all the pools and geysers in the Upper Basin is one known as the Mammoth Paint Pot. The earth surrounding it is cracked and blistered by heat, and from this rises a parapet five feet high, enclosing a space resembling a circus ring. Within this area is a mixture of soft clay and boiling water, suggesting an enormous caldron of hot mush. This bubbling slime is almost as diversely tinted as the pools themselves. It seemed to me that I was looking into a huge vat, where unseen painters were engaged in mixing colors. The fact is easily explained. The mineral ingredients of the volcanic soil produce these different hues. In a new form, it is the same old story of the Mammoth Terraces. Fire supplies the pigments, and hot water uses them. All other features of the Park are solemn and impressive; but the Mammoth Paint Pot provokes a smile. There is no grandeur here. It

THE MAMMOTH PAINT POT.

THE ROAD BY GIBBON RIVER.

"GROTESQUE IMAGES IN CLAY."

seems a burlesque on volcanic power. The steam which oozes through the plastic mass tosses its substance into curious Liliputian shapes, which rise and break like bubbles. A mirthful demon seems to be engaged in molding grotesque images in clay, which turn a somersault, and then fall back to vanish in the seething depths. Now it will be a flower, then a face, then, possibly, a manikin resembling toys for children. Meanwhile one hears constantly a low accompaniment of groanings, hiccoughs, and expectorations, as if the aforesaid demon found this pudding difficult to digest.

ON THE CONTINENTAL DIVIDE.

Soon after leaving the Upper Geyser Basin, we approached a tiny lake which has, in some respects, no equal in the world. With the exception of some isolated mountain peaks, it marks the highest portion of our country. In winter, therefore, when encircled by mounds of snow, it rests upon the summit of our continent like a crown of sapphire set with pearls. So evenly is it balanced, that when it overflows, one part of it descends to the Atlantic, another part to the Pacific. This little streamlet, therefore, is a silver thread connecting two great oceans three thousand miles apart. Accordingly, one might easily fancy that every drop in this pure mountain reservoir possessed a separate individuality, and that a passing breeze or falling leaf might decide its destiny, propelling it with gentle force into a current which should lead it eastward to be silvered by the dawn, or westward to be gilded by the setting sun.

On either side of this elevation, known as the Continental Divide, the view was glorious. In one direction, an ocean of

THE "SILVER THREAD CONNECTING TWO OCEANS."

THE THREE TETONS.

dark pines rolled westward in enormous billows. The silver surfaces of several lakes gleamed here and there like whitecaps on the rolling waves. Far off upon the verge of the horizon, fifty miles away, three snow-capped, sharply pointed mountains looked like a group of icebergs drifting from the Polar Sea. They did not move, however, nor will they move while this old earth shall last. They antedate by ages the Pyramids which they resemble. They will be standing thus, in majesty, when Egypt's royal sepulchres shall have returned to dust. Forever anchored there, those three resplendent peaks rise fourteen thousand feet above the sea, and form the grand tiara of our continent, the loftiest summits of the Rocky Mountains.

As we began the descent from this great elevation, another

splendid vision greeted us. We gazed upon it with delight. Beyond a vast expanse of dark green pines we saw, three hundred feet below us, Lake Yellowstone. It stirred my heart to look at last upon this famous inland sea, nearly eight thousand feet above the ocean level, and to realize that if the White Mountain monarch, Washington, were planted in its

LAKE YELLOWSTONE, FROM A DISTANCE.

depths (its base line on a level with the sea), there would remain two thousand feet of space between its summit and the surface of this lake! In this respect it has but one real rival, Lake Titicaca, in the Andes of Peru.

Descending to the shore, however, we found that even here, so far from shipyards and the sea, a steamboat was awaiting us. Imagine the labor of conveying such a vessel sixty-five

RUSTIC FALLS, YELLOWSTONE PARK.

THE SOLITARY STEAMBOAT.

miles, from the railroad to this lake, up an ascent of more than three thousand feet. Of course, it was brought in several sections; but even then, in one or two mountain gorges, the cliffs had to be blasted away to make room for it to pass. It is needless to add that this steamer has no rivals. It was with the greatest interest that I sailed at such a height on this adventurous craft; and the next time that I stand upon the summit of Mount Washington, and see the fleecy clouds float in the empyrean, one-third of a mile above me, I shall remember that the steamer on Lake Yellowstone sails at precisely the same altitude as that enjoyed by those sun-tinted galleons of the sky.

ON LAKE YELLOWSTONE.

To appreciate the beauty of Lake Yellowstone, one should behold it when its waves are radiant with the sunset glow. It is, however, not only beautiful; it is mysterious. Around it, in the distance, rise silver crested

THE SLEEPING GIANT.

peaks whose melting snow descends to it in ice-cold streams. Still nearer, we behold a girdle of gigantic forests, rarely, if ever, trodden by the foot of man. Oh, the loneliness of this great lake! For eight long months scarcely a human eye beholds it. The wintry storms that sweep its surface find no boats on which to vent their fury. Lake Yellowstone has never mirrored in itself even the frail canoes of painted savages. The only keels that ever furrow it are those of its solitary steamer and some little fishing-boats engaged by tourists. Even these lead a very brief existence. Like summer insects, they float here a few weeks, and disappear, leaving the winds and waves to do their will.

In sailing on this lake, I observed a distant mountain whose summit bore a strange resemblance to an upturned human face, sculptured in bold relief against the sky. It is appropriately called the Sleeping Giant; for it has slept on, undisturbed, while countless centuries have dropped into the gulf of Time, like leaves in the adjoining forest. How many nights have cast their shadows like a veil upon that giant's silhouette! How many dawns have flooded it with light, and found those changeless features still confronting them! We call it human in appearance, and yet that profile was the same before the first man ever trod this planet. Grim, awful model of the coming race, did not its stern lips smile disdainfully at the first human pygmy fashioned in its likeness?

This lake has one peculiarity which, in the minds of certain tourists, eclipses all the rest. I mean its possibilities for fishing. We know that sad experience has taught mankind to invent the proverb: "Once a fisherman, always a liar." I wish, then, at the start, to say I am no fisherman; but what I saw here

ALONG THE SHORE.

would inevitably make me one if I should remain a month or two upon these shores. Lake Yellowstone is the fisherman's paradise. Said one of Izaak Walton's followers to me: "I would rather be an angler here than an angel." Nor is this strange. I saw two men catch from this lake in one hour more than a hundred splendid trout, weighing from one to three pounds apiece! They worked with incredible rapidity. Scarcely did the fly touch the water when the line was drawn, the light rod dipped with graceful curve, and the revolving reel drew in the speckled beauty to the shore. Each of these anglers had two hooks upon his line, and both of them once had two trout hooked at the same time, and landed them; while we poor eastern visitors at first looked on in dumb amazement, and then enthusiastically cheered.

Can the reader bear something still more trying to his faith? Emerging from the lake is a little cone containing a boiling pool, entirely distinct from the surrounding water. I saw a fisherman stand on this and catch a trout, which, without moving from his place, or even unhooking the fish, he

GREAT FISHING.

LARRY, AS FISHERMAN AND COOK.

dropped into the boiling pool, and cooked! When the first scientific explorers of this region were urging upon Congress the necessity of making it a National Park, their statements in regard to fishing were usually received with courteous incredulity. But when one of their number gravely declared that trout could there be caught and boiled in the same lake, within a radius of fifteen feet, the House of Representatives broke forth into roars of laughter, and thought the man a monumental liar. We cannot be surprised, therefore, that enthusiastic fishermen almost go crazy here. I have seen men, after a ride of forty miles, rush off to fish without a moment's rest as if their lives depended on it. Some years ago, General Wade Hampton visited the Park and came as far as Lake Yellowstone. On his return, some one inquired what he thought of Nature's masterpiece, the cañon of the Yellowstone.

"The cañon!" cried the general, "no matter about the cañon; but I had the most magnificent fishing I ever saw in my life."

One day, while walking along the shore, my comrade suddenly pressed my arm and pointed toward the lake. "An Indian!" I cried in great astonishment, "I thought no Indians ever came here." Our guide laughed heartily; and, as he did so, I perceived my error. What I had thought to be an Indian was but a portion of a tree, which had been placed upright against a log. The only artificial thing about it was a bunch of feathers. Everything else was absolutely natural. No knife had sculptured it. No hand had given a support to its uplifted arm. Even the dog which followed us appeared deceived, for he barked furiously at the strange intruder. There was to me a singular fascination in this solitary freak of nature; and, surrounded though I was by immeasurably greater wonders, I turned again and again to take a farewell look at this dark, slender figure, raising its hand, as if in threatening gesture to some unseen foe.

A FALSE ALARM.

Leaving the lake, we presently entered the loveliest portion of the Park, — a level, sheltered area of some fifty square miles, to which has been given the appropriate name of Hayden Valley, in commemoration of the distinguished geologist, Doctor Ferdinand V. Hayden, who did so much to explore this region and to impress upon the Government the necessity of preserving its incomparable natural features. Even this tran-

HAYDEN VALLEY.

APPROACHING THE MUD GEYSER.

quil portion of the Park is undermined by just such fiery forces as are elsewhere visible, but which here manifest themselves in different ways. Thus, in the midst of this natural beauty is a horrible object, known as the Mud Geyser. We crawled up a steep bank, and shudderingly gazed over it into the crater. Forty feet below us, the earth yawned open like a cavernous mouth, from which a long black throat, some six feet in diameter, extended to an unknown depth. This throat was filled with boiling mud, which rose and fell in nauseating gulps, as if some monster were strangling from a slimy paste which all its efforts could not possibly dislodge. Occasionally the sickening mixture would sink from view, as if the tortured wretch had swallowed it. Then we could hear, hundreds of feet below, unearthly retching; and, in a moment, it would all come up again, belched out with an explosive force that hurled a boiling spray of mud so high that we rushed down the slope. A single drop of it would have burned like molten lead. Five minutes of this was enough; and even now, when I reflect that every moment, day and night, the same regurgitation of black slime is going on, I feel as I have often felt, when, on a stormy night at sea, I have tried to sit through a course-dinner on an ocean steamer.

Not far from this perpetually active object is one that has been motionless for ages, — a granite boulder enclosed by trees as by the bars of a gigantic cage. It is a proof that glaciers once plowed through this region, and it was, no doubt, brought hither in the glacial period on a flood of ice, which, melting in this heated basin, left its burden, a grim reminder of how worlds are made. Think what a combination of terrific forces must have been at work here, when the volcanoes were in full activity, and when the mass of ice which then encased our northern world strove to enclose this prison-house of fire within its glacial arms! One of our party remarked that the covering of this seething, boiling area with ice must have been the nearest approach to "hell's freezing over" that our earth has ever seen.

A STRANGER IN THE YELLOWSTONE.

Another striking feature of our National Park is its Petri-

A NATURAL BRIDGE.

fied Forest, where, scattered over a large area, are solitary columns, which once were trunks of trees, but now are solid shafts of agate. The substance of the wood, however, is still apparent, the bark, the worm-holes, and even the rings of growth being distinctly visible; but every fibre has been petrified by the mysterious substitution of a mineral deposit. No doubt these trees were once submerged in a strong mineral solution, tinted with every color of the rainbow. Still, more marvelous to relate, an excavation on the hillside proves that there are eleven layers of such forests, one above another, divided by as many cushions of lava. Think of the ages represented here, during which all these different forests grew, and were successively turned to stone! This, therefore, is another illustration of the conflict between Life and Death. Each was in turn a victor, and rested on his laurels for unnumbered centuries. Life is triumphant now; but who shall say that Death may not again prove conqueror? If not immediately, Death may well be patient. He will rule all this planet in the end.

A PETRIFIED FOREST.

No one can travel through the Yellowstone Park without imagining how it looks in winter. The snowfall is enormous, some drifts in the ravines being hundreds of feet deep, and, owing to the increased supply of water, the geysers throw higher streams. No traveling is possible then except on snow-shoes; and it is with difficulty that some of the Park hotels are reached as late as the middle of May. Of course, in such a frigid atmosphere, the steam arising from the geysers is almost instantly congealed; and eye-witnesses affirm that, in a temperature of forty degrees below zero, the clouds of vapor sent up by Old Faithful rose fully two thousand feet, and were seen ten miles away.

THE PARK IN WINTER.

It can be well imagined that to do much exploration here, in winter, is not alone immensely difficult, but dangerous. In 1887 an expedition was formed, headed by Lieutenant Frederick Schwatka; but, though he was experienced as an Arctic traveler, in three days he advanced only twenty miles, and finally gave out completely. Most of the exploring party turned back with him; but four kept heroically on, one of whom was the photographer, Mr. F. J. Haynes, of St. Paul. Undismayed by Schwatka's failure, he and his comrades bravely persisted in

THE EXPEDITION OF 1887.

their undertaking. For thirty days the mercury never rose higher than ten degrees below zero. Once it marked fifty-two degrees below! Yet these men were obliged to camp out every night, and carry on their shoulders provisions, sleeping-bags, and photographic instruments. But, finally, they triumphed over every obstacle, having in midwinter made a tour of two hundred miles through the Park. Nevertheless, they almost lost their lives in the attempt. At one point, ten thousand feet above the sea, a fearful blizzard overtook them. The cold and wind seemed unendurable, even for an hour, but they endured them for three days. A sharp sleet cut their faces like a rain of needles, and made it perilous to look ahead. Almost dead from sheer exhaustion, they were unable to lie down for fear of freezing; chilled to the bone, they could make no fire; and, although fainting, they had not a mouthful

F. J. HAYNES.

for seventy-two hours. What a terrific chapter for any man to add to the mysterious volume we call life!

One might suppose by this time that all the marvels of our National Park had been described; but, on the contrary, so far is it from being true, that I have yet to mention the most stupendous of them all, — the world-renowned cañon of the Yellowstone. The introduction to this is sublime. It is a waterfall, the height of which is more than twice as great as that of Niagara. To understand the reason for the presence of such a cataract, we should remember that the entire region for miles was once a geyser basin. The river was then near the surface; and has been cutting down the walls of the cañon ever since. The volcanic soil, decomposed by heat, could not resist the constant action of the water. Only a granite bluff at the upper end of the cañon has held firm; and over that the baffled stream now leaps to wreak its vengeance on the weaker foe beneath.

Through a colossal gateway of vast height, yet only seventy feet in breadth, falls the entire volume of the Yellowstone River.

THE CAÑON FROM A DISTANCE.

YELLOWSTONE RIVER ABOVE THE FALLS.

It seems enraged at being suddenly compressed into that narrow space; for, with a roar of anger and defiance and without an instant's hesitation, it leaps into the yawning gulf in one great flood of dazzling foam. When looked upon from a little distance, a clasp of emerald apparently surmounts it, from which descends a spotless robe of ermine, nearly four hundred feet in length. The lower portion is concealed by clouds of mist, which vainly try to climb the surrounding cliffs, like ghosts of submerged mountains striving to escape from their eternal prison. We ask ourselves instinctively: What gives this river its tremendous impetus, and causes it to fill the air with diamond-tinted spray, and send up to the cliffs a ceaseless roar which echoes and reëchoes down the cañon? How awe-inspiring seems the answer to this question, when we think upon it seriously!

THE GREAT FALLS OF THE YELLOWSTONE.

UPPER FALLS OF THE YELLOWSTONE.

The subtle force which draws this torrent down is the same power that holds the planets in their courses, retains the comets in their fearful paths, and guides the movements of the stellar universe. What is this power? We call it gravitation; but why does it invariably act thus with mathematical precision? Who knows? Behind all such phenomena there is a mystery that none can solve. This cataract has a voice. If we could understand it, perhaps we should distinguish, after all, but one word, — *God.*

THE CANON FROM BRINK OF FALLS.

As for the gorge through which this

THE CAÑON FROM GRAND POINT.

river flows, imagine if you can a yawning chasm ten miles long and fifteen hundred feet in depth. Peer into it, and see if you can find the river. Yes, there it lies, one thousand five hundred feet below, a winding path of emerald and alabaster dividing the huge cañon walls. Seen from the summit, it hardly seems to move; but, in reality, it rages like a captive lion springing at its bars. Scarcely a sound of its fierce fury reaches us; yet, could we stand beside it, a quarter of a mile below, its voice would drown our loudest shouts to one another.

Attracted to this river innumerable little streams are trickling down the colored cliffs. They are cascades of boiling water, emerging from the awful reservoir of heat which underlies this laboratory of the Infinite. One of them is a geyser, the liquid shaft of which is scarcely visible, yet in reality is one hundred and fifty feet in height. From all these hot additions to its waves the temperature of the river, even a mile or two beyond the cañon, is twenty degrees higher than at its entrance.

"Are there not other cañons in the world as large as this?" it may be asked.

Yes, but none like this. For, see, instead of sullen granite walls, these sides are radiant with color. Age after age, and æon after æon, hot water has been spreading over these miles of masonry its variegated sediment, like pigments on an artist's palette. Here, for example, is an expanse of yellow one thousand feet in height. Mingled with this are areas of red, resembling jasper. Beside these is a field of lavender, five hundred feet in length, and soft in hue as the down upon a pigeon's breast. No shade is wanting here except the blue, and God replaces that. It is supplied by the o'erspreading canopy of heaven.

DOWN THE CAÑON FROM INSPIRATION POINT.

Yet there is no monotony in these hues. Nature, apparently, has passed along this cañon, touching the rocks capriciously; now staining an entire cliff as red as blood, now tingeing a light pinnacle with green, now spreading over the whole face of a mountain a vast Persian rug. Hence both sides of the cañon present successive miles of Oriental tapes-

BELOW THE UPPER FALLS.

MILES OF COLORED CLIFFS.

try. Moreover, every passing cloud works here almost a miracle; for all the lights and shades that follow one another down this gorge vary its tints as if by magic, and make of it one long kaleidoscope of changing colors.

Nor are these cliffs less wonderful in form than color. The substance of their tinted rocks is delicate. The rain has, therefore, plowed their faces with a million furrows. The wind has carved them like a sculptor's chisel. The lightning's bolts have splintered them, until, mile after mile, they rise in a bewildering variety of architectural forms. Old castles frown above the maddened stream, a thousand times more grand than any ruins on the Rhine. Their towers are five hundred feet in height. Turrets and battlements, portcullises and drawbridges, rise from the deep ravine, sublime and inaccessible; yet they are still a thousand feet below us! What would be the effect could we survey them from the stream itself, within

TEMPLES SCULPTURED BY THE DEITY.

the gloomy crevice of the cañon? Only their size convinces us that they are works of Nature, not of Art. Upon their spires we see a score of eagles' nests. The splendid birds leave these at times, and swoop down toward the stream; not in one mighty plunge, but gracefully, in slow, majestic curves, lower and lower, till we can follow them only through a field-glass, as they alight on trees which look to us like shrubs.

But many of these forms are grander than any castles. In one place is an amphitheatre. Within its curving arms a hundred thousand people could be seated. Its foreground is the emerald river; its drop-curtain the radiant cañon wall. Cathedrals, too, are here, with spires twice as high as those which soar above the minster of Cologne. Fantastic gargoyles stretch out from the parapets. A hundred flying buttresses connect them with the mountain side. From any one of them as many shafts shoot heavenward as statues rise from the Duomo of Milan; and each of these great cañon shrines, instead of stained glass windows, has walls, roof, dome, and pinnacles, one mass of variegated color. The awful grandeur of these temples, sculptured by the Deity, is overpowering. We feel that we must worship here. It is a place where the Finite prays, the Infinite hears, and Immensity looks on.

Two visions of this world stand out within my memory which, though entirely different, I can place side by side in equal rank. They are the Himalayas of India,

THE CAÑON FROM ARTIST POINT.

and the Grand Cañon of the Yellowstone. On neither of them is there any sign of human life. No voice disturbs their solemn stillness. The only sound upon earth's loftiest mountains is the thunder of the avalanche. The only voice within this cañon is the roar of its magnificent cascade. It is well that man must halt upon the borders of this awful chasm. It is no place for man. The Infinite allows him to stand trembling on the brink, look down, and listen spellbound to the anthem of its mighty cataract; but beyond this he may not, cannot go. It is as if Almighty God had kept for His own use one part of His creation, that man might merely gaze upon it, worship, and retire.

INDEX

EXPLANATORY INDEX

The INDEX and the LIST OF ILLUSTRATIONS of all the Lectures will be found in the pages following. For convenience of reference a separate Index and List of Illustrations is given for each Lecture. The Volume and Page where each complete Lecture can be found, and the Index Pages, where can be found the INDEX and the LIST OF ILLUSTRATIONS of each Lecture, are shown below.

INDEX

NORWAY.

SWITZERLAND.

ATHENS.

VENICE.

CONSTANTINOPLE.

JERUSALEM.

EGYPT.

JAPAN, I. AND II.

CHINA.

INDIA, I. AND II.

PASSION PLAY.

THE DRAMA.

SCENES.

CHARACTERS.

PARIS.

LA BELLE FRANCE.

SPAIN.

BERLIN.

VIENNA.

ST. PETERSBURG.

MOSCOW.

THE RHINE.

BELGIUM.

HOLLAND.

MEXICO.

FLORENCE.

NAPLES.

ROME.

SCOTLAND.

ENGLAND.

LONDON.

SOUTHERN CALIFORNIA.

GRAND CAÑON OF THE COLORADO RIVER.

YELLOWSTONE NATIONAL PARK.

LIST OF ILLUSTRATIONS

LIST OF ILLUSTRATIONS

NORWAY.

SWITZERLAND.

ATHENS.

VENICE.

CONSTANTINOPLE.

JERUSALEM.

EGYPT.

JAPAN.

LECTURE I.

JAPAN.

Lecture II.

CHINA.

INDIA.

Lecture I.

INDIA.

Lecture II.

THE PASSION PLAY.

PARIS.

LA BELLE FRANCE.

SPAIN.

BERLIN.

VIENNA.

ST. PETERSBURG.

MOSCOW.

THE RHINE.

BELGIUM.

HOLLAND.

MEXICO.

FLORENCE.

NAPLES.

ROME.

SCOTLAND.

ENGLAND.

LONDON.

SOUTHERN CALIFORNIA.

GRAND CAÑON OF THE COLORADO RIVER.

YELLOWSTONE NATIONAL PARK.